UNTIL WE MET

Janine Alain, highly successful star of the Parisian cabaret world, was really Joanna Allen, an English girl who wanted nothing more than to settle down, loved and wanted, in a home of her own. But how could she ever convince the man she cared for that for this she would willingly sacrifice her career?

UNTIL WE MET

by

ANNE WEALE

MILLS & BOON LIMITED
17-19 FOLEY STREET
LONDON W1A 1DR

First published 1961

This edition 1974

© Anne Weale 1961

ISBN 0 263 71750 X

*Made and Printed in Great Britain by
C. Nicholls & Company Ltd.
The Philips Park Press, Manchester*

CHAPTER ONE

HE was waiting in her dressing-room after the show. He was tall, blond, good-looking—and heir to the de Mansard shipping fortune. But he was the last person she wanted to see tonight, and she was furious with her dresser for admitting him.

"Yves! I thought you were still in New York," she said coolly.

"But you are pleased to have me back?" he asked, taking her hands, smiling. "You have forgiven me for that foolish quarrel between us? Oh, Janine . . . *ma belle Janine* . . . if you knew how I have missed you! These past two weeks have seemed an eternity."

He would have caught her in his arms, but she managed to free her hands and move quickly to the dressing-table. "You have missed your vocation, *mon cher,*" she said lightly. "You should have been an actor."

"Ah, you are sarcastic. You are still very angry with me."

Joanna unscrewed her ear-rings. Tonight, for her final appearance, she had chosen the dragonfly dress. It was a sheath of glistening bronze lamé, so close and clinging that it seemed to be pasted to her body, and from the jewelled shoulder-straps drifted a cloud of golden gauze, as fragile and iridescent as the wings of some beautiful insect.

"Not at all. I only meant that you like to dramatise everything," she said mildly. "Did you have a good trip? Was your business successful?"

"Oh, to the devil with business!" he exclaimed violently. "What does that matter when you are so cruel to me, *mignonne*?"

Joanna bit her lip. "Look, Yves, I'm really very tired tonight. I don't feel I can stand another of these futile arguments," she said wearily.

There was a strained silence. Then Yves took something

from his pocket and laid it on the glass-topped dressing-table.

"I have not come to argue, *petite*," he said swiftly.

Joanna stared at the flat leather jewel case for a moment. Her fingers trembling slightly, she reached for a cigarette. "I think you had better leave—at once!" The words were like splinters of ice.

"But you misunderstand, *chérie*." Reaching over her shoulder, he pressed a catch and the lid of the case flew open.

Inside, on a bed of rich black silk, lay a magnificent emerald necklace, each brilliant green stone surrounded by rose-cut diamonds.

"The de Mansard emeralds are given to every bride," Yves said quietly. "I am asking you to marry me, Janine."

For another long moment Joanna stared blankly at the fabulous jewels. Then, slowly, she raised her head and looked at his reflection in the mirror.

"Oh, *Yves*!" she said huskily. "Oh, Yves—I'm so sorry."

He knelt by the stool and recaptured her shaking hands. For the first time, she saw tenderness as well as passion in his eager blue eyes.

"Don't look so distressed, *ma mie*. It is my own fault that you should think the worst of me," he admitted wryly. "But you see, it was not until I went away that I realised how much you mean to me." And, before she could question or protest, he had drawn her close and was kissing her.

Joanna did not resist him. Still stunned by the shock of his proposal, she was incapable of any positive reaction. But almost at once Yves felt her lack of response and let her go.

"Janine, what is it?" he asked anxiously. "You are not pleased that I——"

A discreet cough from the direction of the door made them both jerk round. A dark-haired man, whom Joanna had never seen before, was standing in the doorway watching them.

"Good evening," he said politely. "I'm sorry to have intruded—but your door wasn't shut, and I did knock." He spoke in French, but with a pronounced English accent.

Yves scrambled to his feet. "Who the devil are you?" he demanded angrily.

The stranger looked past him to Joanna. "My name is Carlyon," he said quietly, in English.

"Do you know this fellow, Janine?" Yves asked her sharply.

Joanna drew in a breath, then shook her head.

"No, we haven't met before," the man agreed casually. "But I think you must have heard of me . . . Miss Allen."

"Oh, the fool must be tipsy," Yves said, in an exasperated undertone. Then, raising his voice, "I'm afraid you are mistaken, *m'sieur*—and patrons are not permitted to come back-stage. Allow me to direct you to the exit."

The Englishman ignored him. "Am I mistaken, Miss Allen?" he asked her, with a subtle emphasis on the surname.

But this time she did not hesitate. "I'm afraid you must be, *m'sieur*. My name is Janine *Alain,* and"—with a slight shrug—"yours means nothing to me."

The stranger's eyes narrowed slightly. He was even taller than Yves, and more powerfully built. Without hearing his voice, she could have mistaken him for a Frenchman, although his eyes were a clear slate grey and curiously arresting against the deep bronze of his skin.

For a moment she was afraid he was going to press the matter and that Yves might not easily eject him. Then, with a gesture of acceptance and a faintly sardonic smile, he said, "My apologies, *mademoiselle*. It seems I was misinformed." And, with a civil nod to Yves, he walked out of the dressing-room and closed the door behind him.

"What extraordinary behaviour! He must either be drunk or deranged," Yves said, frowning. Then, dismissing the incident, "Come, *chérie,* there is not enough privacy here. As soon as you have changed, we will go to my *appartement.* Why, *petite,* you are trembling! Did that stupid oaf frighten you?"

"N-not really. I can't think how he got in here. He must have slipped through the service door." Her voice was strained. "No, please—" as Yves moved to embrace her again—"I must get out of this costume. I wonder where Marie is?"

7

"She has gone home. I told her you wouldn't require her tonight," Yves explained, with a grin.

Joanna disappeared behind the changing screen. "She had strict instructions not to let you in."

"So she said, but I soon persuaded her that you could not possibly have meant such an order seriously."

"You mean you bribed her," Joanna said drily.

He laughed. "Oh, not a bribe, *chérie*—merely a small token of my appreciation of her services to you. Can you extricate yourself from that costume, or shall I help you? After all, if we are soon to be married . . ."

"I can manage, thanks," Joanna said briskly. She had already wriggled out of the narrow lamé sheath and was fastening the sash of a blue wool dressing-gown.

Emerging from the shelter of the screen, she pulled the sequinned combs from her elaborate chignon, bound a cotton bandeau over her hairline and sat down at the dressing-table again.

Lounging in the single shabby armchair, Yves lit a cigarette and watched her peeling off the inch-long false eyelashes and creaming away the heavy stage make-up. The transformation never failed to fascinate him, for he was one of the very few people who knew that there were two Janine Alains—the glamorous sophisticated cabaret artist, and the "real" Janine, the girl he wanted to marry.

At first, it had been Janine, the cabaret star, who had attracted him. He had been escorting some American business associates on a tour of the leading Paris night-spots and, shortly before midnight, they had arrived at the Club Cordiale. Barely concealing his boredom, Yves had given very little attention to the first part of the floor-show. But when the lights had lowered and a single amber spotlight had focused, not on some banal strip-teaser or sobbing torch-singer, but on a willowy auburn-haired girl with beautiful legs and a genuinely lovely singing voice, his interest had quickened. Even before she had ended her first song he had beckoned a waiter and scribbled a note asking her to join his party.

But within a few minutes of her disappearance between the spangled velvet curtains the man had returned to

8

murmur apologetically that Mademoiselle Alain thanked him for his invitation but was otherwise engaged.

In the end she *had* come—but only after Yves had spoken to the proprietor, who had a suitable respect for the powerful name of de Mansard. And it had been a hollow victory because, although she had been perfectly polite to the Americans, Mademoiselle Alain had shown complete indifference to her host's attempts to charm her.

Indifference was new to Yves, and he did not care for it. Puzzled and challenged by her coolness, he determined to break through her detachment. And six weeks later, after he had spent almost every night at the club and bombarded her with flowers and chocolates and a succession of tempting invitations, his campaign was successful. Suddenly, and still without enthusiasm, she gave him her address and consented to spend a Sunday with him.

But when Yves arrived to fetch her—his opulent silver sports coupé looking oddly incongruous outside the cheap artisans' café where, unexpectedly, she lived—there were two surprises awaiting him.

The first was Janine herself. For a moment, as she ran down the stairs to meet him, he almost failed to recognise her.

"Is anything wrong, Monsieur de Mansard?" she had asked gravely, holding out her hand.

It had been one of the rare occasions when Yves's suave assurance had momentarily deserted him. He had even found himself stammering slightly, like any callow schoolboy at his first rendezvous. But how could he have guessed that, away from the cabaret, Janine was another person— a laughing unsophisticated girl who wore home-made cotton sun-dresses and a minimum of cosmetics and whose hair curled loosely round her neck?

The second surprise had been to find that she was bringing a chaperone, a thin pasty-faced boy who lived in a neighbouring house and had been crippled by polio.

"I was sure you wouldn't mind, and it will be such a treat for him," she had explained quickly. "You see, his family are too poor to take him out much, so Jean has been cooped up in their fusty little room all summer,

9

pauvre petit. A day in the sun will do him the world of good."

And strangely enough—after the first spasm of annoyance—Yves had enjoyed himself. Even when he had had to forfeit the intimate little dinner at a sequestered riverside *auberge* because Jean was half asleep, he had not really minded. He was not aware of it then, but for the first time in twenty-six years of being grossly over-indulged he was finding pleasure in pleasing someone else.

Now, waiting for her to finish removing her *maquillage* and looking back over the twelve months he had known her, he admitted to himself that, from that very first Sunday, he had never really expected Janine to conform to the pattern of his previous light-hearted love affairs. Perhaps, deep down, he had been glad of her resistance. Oh, he had not suddenly become so chivalrous that he had not *tried* to have his own way. Before his trip to the States, marriage had never occurred to him. It was not until he was a thousand miles away from her that he had realised how much he missed her—and not only as an amusing companion or a potential conquest, but as an integral part of his life, as someone to be needed always.

While Yves was reviewing the past, Joanna was thinking of the Englishman called Carlyon. How had he traced her? And for what reason?

"You look very serious, *mignonne*. I thought you would be so happy," Yves said suddenly. Then, remembering how she had failed to respond to his kiss before the intruder had burst in, "Janine, you are upset about something. You are worried how my family will receive you?"

Joanna reached for a face tissue and folded it into a pad. "No . . . no, it isn't that," she answered, in a low voice.

"Then what is it, *ma mie*?" he persisted.

"I—I don't know how to tell you," she stammered painfully. "You see, it's that . . . that I can't marry you, Yves."

He stared at her incredulously. Rejection had never occurred to him. If she had told him that the Eiffel Tower had collapsed, he could not have been more thunderstruck. Apart from the fact that he had taken for granted that she was in love with him . . . he was Yves de Mansard, one of the most eligible bachelors in all Paris. Even if he had been short and squat and repulsive, his position and fortune would still have made him a most desirable "catch." Being handsome and witty and gallant, he was not only sought after by every ambitious matron, but was also the secret idol of their more romantic daughters. That he should offer marriage to a girl who sang in a night-club and thereby flout all the most rigid shibboleths of French society—that in itself was startling. To be refused was inconceivable.

"But—why not?" he demanded, at last.

Joanna's mouth trembled. She hated having to hurt him, but there was no choice.

"It would never do, Yves," she said gently. "Apart from what your family and friends would think—and I'm sure they would be horrified—we just aren't right for each other."

"Why not?" he repeated bewilderedly. "Why not, Janine?"

She bent her head. "Because I'm not in love with you, *mon cher*. I thought you knew that. I had no idea you . . . you might become serious about me."

There was a strained silence. Then Yves gave a harsh laugh. "But of course not—why should you think so?" he said sharply. "Naturally you have judged by my reputation, which is certainly not that of a man with honourable intentions. Far from it. I am Yves de Mansard—the notorious roué, the admitted libertine!"

The bitterness of his tone made her flinch. "You know I don't think of you like that," she protested swiftly. "I may have done so at first—but only at first."

His expression did not soften. "Nevertheless, you have not thought me capable of love," he countered grimly.

Joanna looked down at her hands. Without being aware of it, she had torn the tissue into a dozen shreds. "Should I have done?" she asked quietly.

Yves' mouth tightened, but after a moment he leaned back in the chair and said flatly, "No, you are right, *chérie*. I have only known it myself these past few days." He made a wry grimace. "I suppose this is what is known as the irony of fate. For years I have been disengaging myself from *affaires* which became too intense. Now the situation

11

is reversed." He leaned forward again and laid his hand on her arm. "You really mean this, Janine? You are not just pretending a lack of feeling because you are afraid it would be considered a *mésalliance*?"

She put her hand over his and shook her head. "No, Yves, I'm not pretending. If I could love you as you ought to be loved, I wouldn't care what anyone thought."

"And you are very sure that you don't love me?" he asked her softly.

She shook her head. "I wish I did, *mon cher*. I am sure you will make someone very happy."

"Look, why not think about it?" he said persuasively. "I have sprung this on you too suddenly, and you are not yet accustomed to the idea. Instead of going on this absurd visit to Brittany while the club is closed for six weeks, why don't you come with me to Cannes? You have been working too hard, *mignonne*. You need to lie in the sun and relax. In Brittany it will probably rain most of the time and there will be cold winds and no one to amuse you but some dull English tourists."

She coloured slightly. "Are the English so dull?" she asked, in a casual tone.

He shrugged. "I have always found them so. The men are only concerned with football and livestock, and the women, too, are stolid, like vegetables."

Joanna's mouth quirked slightly. She wondered what he would say if she revealed that, legally, she was herself a "vegetable."

Not that she ever thought of herself as being English—at least not since her father had died. And even before that, she and Michael had always spoken French together and followed French habits of life.

If Yves had ever asked about her background, she would have told him the truth. But he had never seemed curious about her past. And now—well, now it was too late.

"You will come with me?" he urged, taking her absent expression as a sign that she was considering his suggestion. "There will be no scandal entailed. The villa is very secluded and there is a private beach, so we shall not be remarked by any gossip columnists." Another aspect

12

occurred to him, and he added seriously, "Believe me, *chérie*, I shall not take advantage of such an arrangement. It will be solely a holiday, and a chance for you to consider the future at leisure. If you do not wish it, I shall not even try to hold your hand."

It was such an improbable assurance for him to give—yet he was so obviously in earnest—that Joanna felt another surge of compassion for him. Poor Yves! It was indeed a cruel irony that, after years of careless philandering, he should finally fall in love with someone who could not love him.

She shook her head. "No, Yves, I can't come with you. It would only make matters worse."

"But, *mignonne*——"

"Oh, please—you must try to accept it. Marriage isn't something that one has to consider, like . . . like a business contract. One has to know instinctively that it is right; and I know that, for us, it is *not* right. It never will be."

Yves's face was bleak. Suddenly, in the space of a few moments, he seemed to have aged ten years.

"So this is goodbye?" he asked, at last.

Joanna's throat ached. "I think it must be," she said huskily. "As a matter of fact, I'm considering going abroad for a while. There is an offer from London which my agent wants me to accept. But, in any case, I shall not be staying on at the Cordiale."

"I see," he said dully. "Then I wish you success, *ma mie*. You have the makings of a great star—unless someone succeeds where I have failed." He managed a crooked grin. "Well, at least we have made up our quarrel so I can drive you home."

"I—I think, if you don't mind, I'll get a taxi tonight, Yves," Joanna said quickly. She was very much afraid she was going to cry. "Oh . . . don't forget this." Closing the leather jewel case, she thrust it into his hands. "Goodbye, *mon cher. Bonne chance*."

His hand gripped hers for an instant and she felt his lips brush her temple. A moment later he had gone.

*   *   *

It was after noon when Joanna woke up the next day. But

since it had been nearly dawn before she had finally fallen asleep, there were still traces of fatigue about her eyes and mouth.

While she was dressing, Madame Dinard came in with hot coffee and *croissants*.

"So! Now you have finished work and will soon be at leisure, *petite*," she said cheerfully, having set the tray on the table beside the window. "It will do you good to lead a normal life for a change, and the sea air will give you some colour."

"You sound as if you'll be glad to get rid of me," Joanna said teasingly.

Marthe Dinard clicked her tongue reprovingly. "Tck! You know very well that is not so. But I *am* concerned for your health. It isn't natural for a girl of your age to live this irregular life, and you have not had a holiday since poor Monsieur Allen was taken from us."

Joanna poured some coffee, her eyes shadowed. It was over four years since Michael Allen's death, but there were still times when she missed him almost intolerably. Indeed, if it had not been for the kindness and generosity of the Dinard family, she sometimes wondered if she would have survived herself. Paris, so gay and romantic from the tourists' points of view, was not a city in which to be nineteen years old, alone and practically destitute.

"You are a fussy old hen, Marthe," she said lightly. "There's nothing the matter with me that a few days' sun-bathing won't cure. After a week of doing nothing, I shall probably be longing to get back. There certainly won't be much night life in a sleepy Breton fishing village."

"A good thing, too, my little owl," the Frenchwoman said briskly. "What are your plans for today?"

"Nothing strenuous. I have to lunch with Gustave Hugo to discuss my next engagement, and then I shall probably do some shopping."

Half an hour later, having carefully disguised her pallor with a skilful make-up, and wearing an extremely chic silk suit, Joanna went down to a café. Tomorrow, in Brittany, she could dispense with such artifices. But today, in Paris, she was still Janine Alain, and it was necessary to appear groomed and elegant.

Monsieur Dinard was wiping his zinc-topped counter as she entered the bar. He had once been a promising boxer and might well have equalled Carpentier, but he had lost his left arm in the final advance on the Somme and had been forced to go into partnership with his father-in-law. The old man was still alive, but he was over ninety and almost blind, so he spent his days sitting in a basket chair outside the café with a tortoiseshell cat on his lap.

"*Bonjour, Papa.* Can you give me some change?" Joanna asked.

Monsieur Dinard put away his duster and came to the old-fashioned till. In spite of his grizzled hair and the shirt-sleeve pinned to his waistcoat, he was still a formidable adversary and, although the *quartier* was not a notably respectable one, there were never any disturbances at the Café Bernadine.

"And where are you going in that charming nonsense of a hat?" he asked, with a twinkle. "Ah, the Crillon, eh? You are flying high, my little pigeon."

Outside the café Joanna paused to speak to the old grandfather, but both he and the cat were asleep. She stopped to pick up the newspaper he had dropped and glanced at the headlines.

"Good morning, Miss Allen. I was beginning to think I must have missed you," a man said quietly.

Joanna drew in a breath, her whole body stiffening. Standing on the pavement, less than an arm's length away from her, was the man named Carlyon.

"What are you doing here?" she asked sharply, instinctively retreating a couple of steps.

"There's no need to look so alarmed. I only want to talk to you," he said mildly. "Perhaps we can sit down and have a coffee together."

Joanna glared at him. "I am sorry, *m'sieur,* but your visit to the club last night does not entitle you to pester the members of the cabaret. If you persist in annoying me I shall be forced to call a *gendarme.*"

"So you still deny that you are Joanna Allen—in spite of that bracelet you are wearing?"

"My bracelet?" Joanna said blankly. "I—I don't know what you're talking about."

15

He smiled slightly. "It's a very unusual design, isn't it?" he went on, in a conversational tone. "As a matter of fact, it's unique. You may not know it, but it was made to a special order for a seventeenth birthday present. The girl's name was Nina Carlyon. She had red hair and some freckles on her nose. She was very like you, in fact."

For a moment longer Joanna continued to glower at him. Then with a shrug of resignation, she said coldly, "All right, Mr. Carlyon—so my name *is* Joanna Allen. That still doesn't give you the right to pester me."

"I have not the least desire to pester you," he replied smoothly. "All I want is ten minutes of your time."

Joanna glanced at her watch. "You'll have to come back later," she said frostily. "I have an important luncheon engagement at one o'clock."

"In that case, we can kill two birds with one stone. I can drive you to your date, and we can talk on the way. My car is just across the square."

Joanna hesitated. To be honest, now that she had been forced to admit her true identity, she was extremely curious to know how the Englishman had found her, and what his object could be.

"Oh, very well," she said ungraciously. "But I hope you can cope with Paris traffic. I'd like to arrive in one piece."

His car was a dark grey saloon, not a new model but in excellent condition, Joanna noticed. "A pretty good auto, but much too sedate for me," Yves had once remarked of a similar English car.

Yet there was nothing particularly sedate about this Carlyon man, thought Joanna, as he slid behind the steering wheel. It was possible that, meeting him without prejudice, she might even have found him attractive.

"Where do you want me to drop you?" he asked, when they had left the square and were heading towards the river.

"The Crillon, please." Joanna began to give him directions.

He cut her short. "I know where it is, thanks."

"You've been to Paris before?"

He nodded, his attention on the road. "You know," he

said presently, "I expected a certain amount of hostility; but not that you would refuse to admit who you were. Why all the denials?"

"Why not?" Joanna said coldly. "For all practical purposes I am Janine Alain."

"Is that how you think of yourself when you are alone? As Janine—a French girl?"

His percipience nettled her. "We've only a few minutes. You'd better state your business, Mr. Carlyon," she said curtly.

They had stopped at some traffic lights, and she felt him watching her. "You puzzle me," he said speculatively. "I thought you would be interested in us. Isn't it rather intriguing to have a family you've never even met?"

Joanna shrugged. "I've been told all I want to know, thanks."

"But not everything, I fancy," he retorted. "For instance, how much do you know about your grandmother?"

"Not a great deal," Joanna admitted, in a bored tone. "She was the only one who didn't loathe my father, wasn't she?"

"So presumably you bear her less of a grudge."

"I don't bear a grudge against any of you. I've scarcely ever thought of you."

He let that pass. "You know that it was your grandfather who forced the break with your parents?"

"Yes. He must have been a most detestable man," she said scathingly.

"Your grandmother never saw your mother after her marriage," Carlyon continued, again ignoring her comment. "But she knew that you had been born, and she has always hoped to see you. Naturally, as long as her husband was alive, any contact was impossible. But he has been dead for nearly two years now, and since she was widowed she has made every effort to trace you. She's in her seventies now, and she has a serious heart condition. It would mean a great deal to her to see you before she dies."

Joanna gaped at him. "You mean you expect me to visit her?" she demanded incredulously.

17

"I think it would be a charitable thing to do," he said gravely.

For a moment she was too staggered by his effrontery to be capable of speech. Then all her suppressed resentment erupted into words.

"Charitable!" she burst out violently. "Why should I be charitable, Mr. Carlyon? Was it charitable to disown my mother because she was so wicked as to fall in love with an artist? Was it charitable to return my father's letter when he was left with a tiny baby on his hands? Don't talk to me about charity! You don't know the meaning of the word."

Carlyon swung the car into a side-street and braked. Then, switching off the engine, he turned to face her.

"So you aren't as detached as you pretended," he said drily.

Joanna reached for the door, but before she could turn the handle he had caught her other arm and was holding her back.

"Now don't lose your temper," he said quietly. "I agree that your grandfather behaved with extraordinary harshness and that you're bound to feel bitter, even vindictive. But it wasn't your grandmother's fault, and she has suffered as much as anyone."

"Then why didn't she do something about it?" Joanna countered angrily. "*She* could have written to my mother. *She* could have answered Michael's letters."

"Could she?" he said wryly. "I don't think you really understand the matter. She was married to a man of an unusually despotic temperament, and there were certain reasons why she felt she must always be loyal to him— even if it meant denying her deepest convictions. Don't judge her too arbitrarily, Joanna. It was a damnable situation and she had to make the best of it."

He had relaxed his hold on her wrist, and Joanna shook off his hand and rubbed the reddened skin.

"You're a persuasive advocate, Mr. Carlyon, but you're wasting your breath. Even if I wanted to meet your family, it wouldn't be possible. You seem to forget that I have a living to earn. I can't jaunt off to England at a moment's notice."

18

"But I was told that the Cordiale was closing down for a spell and that the artists were going on holiday. I should have thought it was a singularly suitable moment for me to have found you," he said reasonably.

Joanna was unable to repress her curiosity. "How did you find me?" she asked distantly.

"Purely by chance, as it happens. Some friends took me to the Cordiale, and I was struck by your likeness to a painting of your mother. She was wearing that bracelet when she sat for the portrait, so when you came near our table and I recognised the design—well, it was fairly obvious, wasn't it? Especially as your stage name is so like your real one."

Joanna looked down at the broad gold band on her wrist. It was set with three square-cut amethysts and very beautifully engraved, with an intricate clasp and safety chain. Her father had given it to her on her fifteenth birthday, with her mother's pearls and a valuable sapphire brooch. In the dark days after his death, she had been forced to sell both the pearls and the brooch, but she had clung to the bracelet as a kind of talisman. She wore it always.

"I see," she said slowly. "You must be very observant. Most men don't notice such details." Then, with a level glance, "Now, may we get on, please? It's almost one o'clock."

He frowned. "You mean you refuse even to consider the idea?"

"That's right," she said negligently. "The past is past, Mr. Carlyon. There's nothing to be gained by raking over the ashes. As you see, I've made a new life for myself, and I mean to stick to it. As far as I'm concerned, your family doesn't exist."

Carlyon put his hand on the ignition key, but he did not turn it. "Are you really so hard-boiled?" he asked drily.

She shrugged. "It's no use being soft when one has a living to make—particularly in my job."

"I suppose not. Still, you seem to be pretty successful."

Joanna's mouth tightened. "Success doesn't come easily, I'm afraid. There's no time for sentiment if one wants to get to the top."

"And when you get there? What then?" he asked curiously.

"Then I'll find myself a rich husband and relax for the rest of my life," she retorted in a brittle tone. "I don't think Mrs. Carlyon would like me, you know. I'm not one of your sweet docile English girls."

Carlyon's face hardened. "All right, since it's obviously no use appealing to your human instincts, I'll put it in terms that might move you," he said curtly. "How much do you want?" Then, since she appeared not to understand him: "What is your price, *mademoiselle*? How much money would make it worth your while to come to England with me?"

The scorn in his voice brought a flush of indignant colour to her cheeks. But, on the verge of snapping back a furious repudiation, she checked herself. How typical of a Carlyon to think that, when other means failed, there was the offer of their money to achieve an object. Her grandfather had tried to buy Michael off.

"How much can you afford?" she said disdainfully.

"You name it—I'll pay it."

Joanna's temper flared. No wonder her father had hated them, she thought contemptuously. But her face was without expression as she said, "How long would you expect me to stay?"

"That depends on how long you can hide your true colours. I don't want your grandmother to realise that she's been wasting her anxiety over you."

"Oh, I'm quite a good actress, you know. Would a fortnight do?"

"I suppose so," he said tersely.

"Then, for a two-week engagement, my fee would be five hundred pounds—apart from expenses, of course."

Even then, she didn't really believe that he would take her seriously. Five hundred pounds to spend two weeks in England was sheer fantasy. Even if he could afford it, that ice-cold Carlyon pride would never submit to such extortion. With secret derision, she waited for him to start blustering.

Carlyon switched on the engine. "Very well," he said

calmly. "Five hundred, and all expenses. We'll leave first thing tomorrow."

Joanna gasped. "Oh, now, wait a moment——" she began defensively.

The car slid forward, gathering speed. "You'll be five minutes late for your appointment, but I don't think the time has been wasted," he said mockingly. "I'll ring you up this evening and let you know what time I can collect you. Your passport is in order, I suppose?"

"Why, yes, but——"

"Good. I'm afraid you won't be able to bring more than a couple of suitcases, but then you won't need a large wardrobe in Merefield. It's quite a prosperous place these days, but the women are pretty conservative in their dress."

"But I haven't agreed to come," Joanna burst out urgently.

Carlyon glanced at her, and his smile was not pleasant.

"No—but with five hundred pounds at stake, I don't think you'll hesitate for long. You can think it over while you're lunching."

Almost before Joanna realised they had reached her destination, the car was at a standstill and a liveried doorman was waiting to hand her on to the pavement.

"Off you go. I'll telephone you at eight," Carlyon said crisply.

And before she had time to utter any further protests, the saloon was sliding away from her.

*　　　*　　　*

To a casual observer Gustave Hugo was so unprepossessing as to be almost repulsive. The first time Janine had seen him staring at her—she had been working in one of the more dubious Left Bank *caves,* and despairing of ever escaping from it—she had felt an involuntary shiver of repugnance. Even when she had verified that he was indeed *the* Gustave Hugo and that, unbelievably, he was willing to help her, she had had to suppress an instinctive aversion to him. It was only gradually that she came to understand that his gross physique and coarse features were utterly at variance with his character. He was not only the best theatrical agent in Paris, with a sixth sense that enabled

21

him to detect latent talent where none was apparent to others, but he was also a most charming and cultivated man.

As she grew to know him—and to be even more grateful for his expert advice and encouragement—Joanna was reminded of the harmless but horrifying Beast in the old fairy-tale. Only there could never be any magical transformation for Gustave Hugo, and a woman would have to love him with an extraordinary passion to be unconscious of his ugliness.

He was waiting for her in a corner of the cocktail bar as Joanna entered the Crillon ; a bull-shouldered hulk of a man with one hairy hand knotted round a thick Havana cigar and the other thrust into his pocket. Although he went to London for his suits, the most expert tailor could never disguise the ungainliness of his girth, and his pockets were always misshapen by cigars and pens and other impedimenta. Grotesquely magnified by the specially thick lenses of his spectacles, his shrewd dark eyes ranged over the other occupants of the lounge.

"Ah, Janine—tu es arrivée!" Seeing her approach, Hugo heaved himself out of his chair and kissed her hand. "Now what will you take before lunch? No, no—not one of your insipid fruit juices today, *ma petite*. Today is an occasion—a milestone! Let me consider—ah yes, a champagne cocktail would be most appropriate. I am sure one glass will not impair that charming complexion of which you take so much care, and one cannot toast the future in a grenadine."

"I'm sorry I'm late, Gustave," Joanna apologised, when he had given the order.

She leaned back against the luxurious silk upholstery of the couch to which he had ushered her, and slowly stripped off her gloves. She had been so unnerved by her encounter with the Englishman that she had only half heard the agent's effusive greeting and was still preoccupied.

Indeed it was not until she had smoothed out her gloves and laid them on the seat beside her, and the waiter was setting down her drink, that she realised that Gustave had been explaining something.

"So you agree to these arrangements?" he enquired.

Joanna flushed crimson. "Oh, Gustave, I *am* so sorry.

22

I didn't mean to be rude, but I was thinking of . . . of something else."

"Something very absorbing, I imagine, if you are so *distraite* that you fail to hear my own good tidings," he said drily. "I am intrigued, *petite*. What can it be that causes such deep abstraction?"

Joanna picked up the champagne glass and watched the bubbles rising to the surface of the pale golden liquid. "Oh, nothing so very important," she said, with a shrug. "I'll tell you about it later. Now, what were you saying while I so rudely ignored you?"

"Ah, that was *very* important," he explained with satisfaction. "As you know, I have been exploring the possibilities of your appearing in London for a season. Well, matters have turned out even better than I anticipated. There has been an offer from one of the most exclusive cabarets, and their terms are excellent—excellent! What is more, there will be at least two engagements in top-rating television productions, and more than likely an appearance in one of the gala variety programmes. So it is certainly an occasion for us to congratulate ourselves, don't you think?"

"It sounds wonderful, Gustave," she said breathlessly. "But it will be much more exacting than my run at the Cordiale. Are you sure I'm ready for it?"

"If you are not, then it will be the first time I have miscalculated," he said drily. "Yes, you are ready, Janine. You will have to prepare yourself, of course—it will need much hard work—but you are ready."

He smoked his cigar for a moment his expression reflective. "You see, *ma petite*," he said slowly, "it is not really a question of your voice—which is charming; or your appearance—which is delightful. There are dozens of girls who have both assets. No, it is something less tangible, something which one can only describe as . . . magic. If you have it, you cannot fail! If you do not have it—" he made an expressive gesture—"then you may be extremely successful, but never a great star."

He had always encouraged and spurred her, but he had never told her that she might reach the very pinnacles of success. Joanna was rather overwhelmed.

"But what makes you think I might have this . . . magic, Gustave?" she asked doubtfully. "After all, I seemed to be reasonably popular at the Cordiale, but there were never any queues."

"Because, at the Cordiale, you were still serving your apprenticeship . . . still learning," he said wisely. "A great artist—one who will last for a lifetime—such a rarity does not emerge overnight, Janine. But there is always one moment when, afterwards, one can say 'That was the beginning—that was the great moment.' It was true of Mistinguette, and of the enchanting Josephine Baker, and, more recently, of Piaf. And if my hopes are fulfilled, it will be true of you, my little one. So now we drink a toast—yes? To Janine Alain—and to a golden future."

During lunch, they discussed the more practical details of the London project. But it was not until the waiter had poured their coffee and most of the other diners had left the restaurant that Gustave said quietly, "And now I should like to know what has occurred to distress you, *petite*. Oh, yes, I can see that you are not quite yourself today. Even though you are pleased and excited about this venture, there is still something troubling you."

Since it had never been any use trying to hide anything from him—and as he already knew the whole story of her upbringing—Joanna told him what had happened. But, for reasons which she could not quite define, she omitted any mention of the money Carlyon had offered her.

To her astonishment, Gustave was immediately in favour of the visit.

"Why not? Why not, *ma chère*?" he asked, with a wave of his cigar. "If you are truthful with yourself, I think you must admit that you have always been curious about these unknown relatives of yours. You have every reason to dislike them, yet there is still this subconscious hankering to observe them for yourself. Once you have met them, this feeling will be satisfied and the past will no longer weigh so heavily." He sipped his cognac. "And, what is more, it will be an excellent opportunity for you to familiarise yourself with the English way of life before making your début," he added approvingly.

"But, Gustave, he wants me to leave tomorrow," Joanna objected.

"So? You can be ready, can you not? It is a simple matter to cancel your arrangements in Brittany. As for your appearance in London, these Carlyons must surely have a telephone, or I can advise you by letter. In any event, I shall be coming to London to supervise your opening myself."

"You will? Oh, that will make all the difference. I shan't be half so nervous if you are there," Joanna said, with relief.

"So it is agreed that you accompany this Englishman?" the agent asked briskly.

Joanna nodded. "I suppose so—if you think I should."

Hugo patted her hand. "Don't look so nervous, little goose. They cannot eat you. And now I must return to my office. I can give you a lift, perhaps?"

"No, I think I'll walk for a while, thank you."

"There is one person who will not be overjoyed at your departure, I fancy," Gustave said casually, when he had signed the bill and the *maître* had bowed them out of the dining-room. Then, as she gave him an enquiring glance, "I mean young de Mansard."

Joanna was taken aback. She had had no idea that the agent was aware of her association with Yves. He had certainly never seen them together.

"Oh, yes, I have known of his interest in you," Gustave said, correctly interpreting her expression. "To be frank with you, *chérie,* I was at one time a little concerned by it. Contrary to some opinions, I do not consider that *all* publicity is advantageous."

"You never said anything," Joanna said curiously.

He chuckled. "No—but I would if it had been necessary. Fortunately, you were both extremely discreet."

There was nothing in his tone to warrant it, but Joanna felt bound to say, "There was nothing to be discreet about, Gustave. We were only friends."

"I am sure of it, *petite*—but few others would be. You must know of his reputation."

"Yes, I do—and at first I didn't like him," Joanna admitted.

"And now?" the agent enquired.

She hesitated, wondering whether to tell him that she would not be seeing Yves again. Instead, she said, "What made you so sure that I wouldn't become . . . involved with him?"

Gustave smiled slightly. "Because for you, *mon enfant*, there would be no involvement without love; and you have not yet experienced that condition. It is, perhaps, your one imperfection as an *artiste*."

"Falling in love?" she exclaimed. "But what has that to do with my work?"

"A very great deal," he said drily. "Until you have loved, you are not completely a woman—the deepest emotions are unknown to you. However, I don't doubt that it is a lack which will shortly be remedied. Perhaps one of your compatriots will introduce you to the experience. You will find that Englishmen are not always the dull fellows they are sometimes made out to be."

His gleaming Delahaye was waiting outside the entrance when they emerged from the hotel. The chauffeur, who had been chatting to the doorman, sprang to open the door and saluted Janine.

"So the next time we meet will be in London—to prepare for your triumph," Gustave said, with a chuckle. *"Au revoir, ma petite.* Take good care of yourself."

Joanna gave him her hand. "Bless you, Gustave. Where should I be without you?" she said warmly. And then, on impulse, she leaned forward and brushed her lips against his fleshy cheek. *"Au revoir,* my good friend."

The agent watched her walk away, a slim graceful figure, her red-gold hair burnished by the afternoon sun. Then he heaved himself into the limousine and gave his instructions to the chauffeur.

Joanna would never know it, but if they had been characters in a fairy-tale, it would have been a handsome young prince who was driven swiftly away.

*   *   *

Joanna was packing her suitcases when Madame Dinard shouted up the stairs that there was a gentleman on the telephone. It was exactly one minute past eight.

"Well? Have you made up your mind?" From halfway across the city, Charles Carlyon's voice was even more cold and incisive than when they had talked in his car.

Joanna's fingers trembled as she held the receiver to her ear and tried to shut out the babel of chattering voices from the bar. But her tone was as crisp as his as she answered, "Yes, Mr. Carlyon. I've decided to accept your invitation."

"I thought you would. I'll pick you up at eight o'clock tomorrow. We shall be catching the noon boat from Calais, so try not to keep me waiting."

"I'll be ready," she said icily.

"Oh, and there's one other point. Don't think your five hundred pounds is going to be easy money. You've got a part to play, and it certainly isn't type-casting. One slip, my dear Joanna, and you'll wish you'd never been born. Good-night."

CHAPTER TWO

BY ten minutes past eight the following morning, Joanna's luggage had been fitted into the boot of Charles Carlyon's car, and he was waiting for her to take her leave of the Dinards.

Although she had told the French family that she was leaving the Cordiale and appearing in London for a season, she had not mentioned the immediate alteration in her plans. They were under the impression that Carlyon was a friend who had offered to drive her to the coast.

"Il est tout à fait charmant, this new *beau,"* Madame Dinard whispered, as they kissed goodbye. "Perhaps he will also decide to spend some time in Brittany," she added archly.

Joanna managed a smile. She had been relieved when the Englishman had given no sign of his disdain for her while they were arranging her suitcases. But she had not the least doubt that his pleasant manner was only a temporary front, and that, once on the road, he would swiftly dispense with all hypocrisy.

At the last moment, just as he was about to start the engine, Papa Dinard clapped his hand to his forehead and called a halt.

"Forgive me, little one," he said apologetically, having disappeared into the bar for some moments and returned with a small package. "I had completely forgotten that this parcel was delivered for you yesterday. I put it under the counter, but what with Marthe cutting herself on the bread knife, and the old man being in one of his fractious tempers, it completely slipped my memory."

Joanna took the flat wax-sealed packet with a puzzled expression. She had no idea what it could be as she had certainly not ordered anything from the shops in the past few days.

"Oh, I don't suppose it's anything important, Papa," she

said lightly. "Perhaps something I left behind at the club." Then, as the car moved forward: *"Au'voir, Papa. Au'voir, Maman.* Take care of yourselves."

It was not until they had left the central part of the city and were passing through the quieter streets of the suburbs that Carlyon broke the silence by glancing at the packet on her lap and saying, "Aren't you going to open it? It may be a farewell gift from one of your admirers."

"I doubt it," Joanna said coolly. "It may be a small present from my agent, Monsieur Hugo. He is almost the only person who knows my private address."

"I should have thought you would have an *appartement,"* Carlyon said casually, as she broke the seals. "Or is it a publicity gimmick to live in a back-street café?"

"I live with the Dinards because they were very kind to me when I was having . . . difficulties," Joanna said flatly. "I'm comfortable there, and I like them."

Opening the thick white wrapping paper, she found that the packet was a small shagreen box in a transparent slip-over. The name of a leading Paris jeweller was stamped in gold on the cellophane. If it had not been so early in the day, she might have had the quickness of wit to say carelessly, "Oh, yes, of course—the bracelet I sent to be mended," and tuck it away in her bag. Instead, to her subsequent embarrassment, she removed the protective wrapper and opened the case.

Even then, she could have covered her mistake if it had not been for the road block. Carlyon, who had seen the red flags from a distance and reduced speed, now brought the car to a halt. So there was no question of the glitter of expensive stones and Joanna's muffled exclamation escaping his attention.

His eyebrows shot up as he saw the exquisite sapphire ear-clips lying on their satin bed. "Your agent must think very highly of you," he said drily.

Joanna's face flamed, and she closed the case with a snap. "It was not from Gustave after all," she said repressively.

"From the ardent young man with the emeralds, perhaps," Carlyon suggested, without expression. He bent to retrieve something from the floor. "His card, I imagine."

Joanna controlled an impulse to snatch it from his hand and thrust it in her pocket. As composedly as she could manage, she read the brief message. There was no signature, but she had instantly recognised Yves's sprawling hand. *'A memento of an enchanting interlude,'* he had written.

"Was I right?" Carlyon asked smoothly.

Joanna gave him a single withering glance. "You should have been a detective," she said frigidly. "Does *anything* escape your eagle eye?"

"I would be very unobservant not to have noticed the small fortune that was lying on your dressing-table the other night," he replied, quite unabashed. "It could have been paste, I suppose—but those ear-rings certainly aren't. They must be worth even more than your fee for this fortnight in England."

Joanna didn't answer him, and stared stonily out of the window. Last night, shifting restlessly about her single bed, she had made up her mind to tell him the truth—to admit that she had only taken up his offer of money because she was angry and upset. She had even been ready to suggest that they should try to forget their bad start and call a truce. But now, she not only felt more antagonistic than before, but was convinced that such an attempt would have been wasted.

They were still held up at the block, for a long section of the outward roadway was being re-laid and a steady stream of cars was heading for the city. Carlyon switched off the engine and offered her a cigarette.

"No, thank you. I don't smoke," Joanna said coldly.

"You're certainly very thorough," he said presently.

"In what way?"

"In dressing the part. If I hadn't picked you up at the café, I might not have recognised you."

"What did you expect, Mr. Carlyon? Fish-net stockings and a startling décolletage?" she enquired derisively.

"Not at all," he said mildly. "I'm sure your taste is always excellent. But yesterday you were a fashion-plate, and today . . ." He concluded the sentence with a gesture.

Joanna glanced down at her olive linen slacks. They

30

seemed the most sensible thing to wear on what might be a blowy Channel crossing, and, because it was still early in the day, she had a light olive sweater over her cream silk shirt.

"Yesterday I was Janine Alain. Today . . . I am whatever you want me to be," she answered indifferently.

Nevertheless it vexed her that he should assume she was already playing a part. Obviously he would never believe that she always wore casual clothes for her private life, or that it was not exceptional for her skin to be free of make-up except for a light dusting of powder and some coral lipstick.

Perhaps he imagines that I rushed out and bought myself a whole wardrobe of *ingénue* clothes, she thought sardonically. Oh, bother the man! I don't care what he thinks.

The last of the oncoming cars was passing the barrier now, and Carlyon reached for the ignition key.

"Oh, by the way, my first name is Charles," he remarked. "Distasteful as it may be to you, I think you'd better use it." And, with a rather mocking smile, he signalled he was pulling out and returned his attention to the road.

Joanna did not reply. Presently she took a magazine from her capacious straw carry-all and gave every appearance of being deeply absorbed in it.

It was a little after ten, and they were in the outskirts of Rouen, when he pulled up outside a hotel and suggested a short break. Now that the sun was high it was very warm, so they sat at a table in the courtyard and Charles ordered coffee and *brioches*. While they were waiting, Joanna took off her sweater and rolled up the sleeves of her shirt. In spite of her Titian hair, her complexion had never been too sensitive for sun-bathing and she was lightly tanned. But compared with Charles's gypsy-dark colouring, her arms looked quite pale.

"Have you been on holiday?" she asked, since she was bound to speak to him at some point.

He nodded. "I've been down in Provence for a fortnight. It was a last-minute decision to spend a couple of nights in Paris and take in some of the night spots."

"I should have thought the opera or a concert would have been more in your line," she said mildly.

He arched an eyebrow. "Is that a jibe?" he enquired.

"Not at all. You just don't look the cabaret type."

"Which you would prefer, no doubt."

Joanna shrugged. "As you prefer the sheltered English rose type, I imagine."

His eyes narrowed slightly. "Perhaps," he said negligently. Then, after appraising her thoughtfully for some moments, "I wonder how you'll get on with Vanessa."

The waiter was bringing their coffee, so Joanna waited until they were alone again. "Who is Vanessa?" she asked.

"Oh, of course, you wouldn't know about her. She is one of your cousins. You knew your mother had a sister, I suppose?"

"Yes, Michael told me about her. She was several years the younger and they were quite unalike, he said. I did know her name, but I've forgotten it."

"Monica," Charles supplied. "Monica Durrant. Her husband died several years ago and, since then, she and the children have lived at Mere House with your grandmother."

"How many children are there?" Joanna asked.

"Three—but they're not really children now. Neal is twenty-five and works in the family business. Vanessa's twenty-three, and Cathy is just sixteen. She's still at school, of course."

Joanna buttered a *brioche* and began to eat it. She had been too on edge to eat much earlier on, and was now very hungry.

"What does Vanessa do?" she queried presently.

"What work, d'you mean? She hasn't a job. She helps her mother run the house."

"Isn't that dull for her?" Joanna asked.

She knew very little about the way in which English girls lived, but she had supposed that nowadays even the wealthier ones had some kind of career.

"I shouldn't think so," Charles replied, as if the possibility had never occurred to him before. "She's a very domesticated girl, and with the difficulty of getting capable staff and your grandmother being a semi-invalid, there's plenty for her to do."

He lit a cigarette, missing the slight grimace that twisted Joanna's soft lips. Somehow she didn't much like the sound of her cousin Vanessa.

"Aren't you afraid that I may corrupt her?" she asked, with a gleam of mischief.

Charles crossed his long legs and leaned back in the sun-bleached basket chair.

"I'm hoping that she may have an improving influence on you," he said blandly.

It was only a thrust, of course—and she had left herself open to it—but she felt herself flushing slightly.

"And what is *our* relationship?" she asked quickly.

"An extremely remote one, you'll be glad to hear. My grandfather and yours were stepbrothers."

"Do you live at Mere House too?"

He shook his head. "No, I have a place of my own—but it isn't far away. Now that your grandfather is dead, I run the family business."

A thought occurred to her. "Are you married, Charles?"

"If I were, my wife would be with me," he said drily.

"Oh, not necessarily. I believe people often go on holiday separately nowadays."

"So one hears, but that isn't my idea of marriage."

Joanna glanced at him. Her father was the only Englishman that she had ever known well, and she had heard that they made excellent husbands but indifferent lovers. But in Charles Carlyon's case—from what little she knew of him so far—she would have supposed the reverse to be true. Physically, as she had already had to concede, he was extremely attractive—if one had a weakness for that particular type of aggressively masculine magnetism. But as a husband, she was sure he would be insufferable. He was so sure of himself, so arrogant.

"How are you going to explain me to the neighbourhood?" she asked, when they were driving on again. "Do they know the true story, or will you think up some

33

respectable explanation of why I've never been to Mere House before?"

"Many of the older people knew your mother, and I dare say the rest have heard a garbled version of what happened."

"I see. Well, at least my arrival will give them something to gossip about," she said carelessly.

They reached Calais an hour before the ferry was due to leave, and Charles left her in the car while he went to arrange her passage. The weather was changing. It was still sunny, but a gusty wind had blown up and there were cloud banks on the horizon.

"Have you been to sea before? It may be fairly choppy," he said, as they waited in a queue of cars to pass through the Customs sheds.

Joanna smiled to herself. "I shan't mind that," she said briefly.

"What's the joke?" he asked.

"Nothing, really. Your question was rather amusing in the circumstances, but you can't be expected to know the kind of life we led when my father was alive."

"What kind of life did you lead?" he asked, studying her profile.

She shrugged, turned her head to follow the flight of a sea-gull. If he could have seen her eyes, he might have detected a flicker of remembered heartache in them.

"Michael once said that if he ever wrote his memoirs he would call then 'Here Today and Gone Tomorrow'," she said carelessly. "That was just how we lived—like nomads. I had my ninth birthday in Rio, and my tenth in Lisbon. When I reached eleven, we were somewhere in the Indian Ocean."

The queue of cars began to move and he quickly switched on the engine and edged the car forward. There were not many people travelling, and those who were made for the shelter of the bar.

"Shall we have a drink?" Charles suggested, as they emerged from the car-hold.

Joanna tied a silk scarf over her hair and slipped on a pair of sun-glasses.

"If you don't mind, I'd like to be alone for a while. You go inside if you want to. I'll stay on deck," she said politely.

Charles hesitated, frowning. Then he said, "As you wish," and walked to the entrance to the saloon.

Left to herself, Joanna wandered about the forward deck, the wind whipping her slacks and blowing keenly against her cheeks. It was a long time since she had smelt the sharp freshness of sea air and heard the waves slapping against a hull.

It must have been nearly an hour later, and her thoughts were far away, when a light touch on her shoulders roused her. Turning, she found Charles at her elbow.

"Come inside and have lunch. You must be hungry," he said. The wind had loosened her scarf, and as she moved to follow him a strong gust snatched at the thin silk and almost blew it free.

Joanna gave a startled exclamation and put up her hands, but Charles was quicker, and before a second gust could carry it away he had reach out and caught it and, with it, a skein of her hair.

"Thank you. I should have knotted it," she said breathlessly, taking it from him and trying to smooth the flying tangle about her face.

"You should have a coat," he said. "Didn't you bring one?"

"Yes, it's in my case. But I'm not cold. I love the wind."

They crossed the deck and passed into the covered way leading to the dining-room. Joanna opened her bag and hunted for a comb and mirror.

"I shan't be a minute. I can't have lunch looking like a haystack," she said.

"Here, let me hold the glass for you," he said, taking it.

It took her only a few seconds to restore her hair to order, but when she thanked him and took back the mirror, she found him watching her with an odd expression.

"What's the matter?" she asked.

"I was thinking that you're not at all like Janine Alain

35

at the moment," he said. "It suits you—your hair blowing about and colour in your cheeks." But his eyes were mocking.

"It's only a sea-change," she said carelessly.

The dining-room was almost empty, as the ferry was rolling more strongly now and many of the passengers had retreated below decks. "What is this business of yours?" Joanna asked, as the steward brought their soup.

"A shoe factory. I suppose that sounds pretty dull to you."

"Oh, no. I love shoes. They're my worst extravagance," she said pleasantly. "What kind do you make? Fashionable ones, or the serviceable kind?"

"Mainly fashion shoes, but we also make children's shoes and some specialist lines such as ballet slippers and certain types of sports footwear. If you're really interested, I'll take you round the factory some time."

"Yes, I am. I should love to see it," she said sincerely. "I've never had any English shoes. The ones I'm wearing are Belgian."

"Yes, I thought they were. The Belgians are first-class craftsmen and they can sell much more cheaply than we can," he told her.

"Did you want to take over the factory, or did you have to?" she asked.

"Fortunately I wanted to," he said. "It's Neal who dislikes it. He works in our design section, but he fancies himself as a serious artist and doesn't take kindly to commercialising his talents."

"Must he?" she asked.

"He isn't forced to stay with us, but he's not prepared to rough it while he makes his name," Charles said drily. "He's been spoilt a good deal by his mother and thinks he should have a directorship to support him while he turns out a masterpiece. However, I expect he'll tell you his troubles himself. He has a weakness for attractive women."

"While you, no doubt, are proof against the most alluring creatures," Joanna remarked sweetly.

Charles eyed her sardonically. "Experience tends to reduce one's susceptibility," he agreed coolly.

Joanna waited for the steward to whisk away their soup plates and serve the roast meat. Then she said, "Have you had a great deal of experience?"

"Enough to know most of the devices by which your sex gain their ends," he said negligently.

"Really? I should have thought you'd have been too busy with business matters to make a study of us."

"I allow a certain amount of time for the lighter side of life," he said carelessly. "You'll find that Englishmen don't take women as seriously as the French do."

"No, so I've heard," Joanna said drily. "You're more interested in horses or football, I believe. No doubt that's why my mother ran off with an artist."

By the time they had finished their meal, it had begun to drizzle, so she was obliged to accompany Charles to the lounge.

"What will you have to drink?" he asked. "Gin and something?"

"I'd like a tomato juice, please, if they have it."

His lips quirked. "Oh, come now, you don't have to restrict yourself to that extent. A gin and orange is quite permissible at your age."

"Possibly, but I never drink spirits. They spoil one's skin and I can't afford to risk losing any of my assets," she said crisply.

It was raining fairly heavily when they arrived at the hotel in Dover where Charles proposed to spend the night. Waiting while he signed the register, Joanna felt tired and chilled and very much an alien.

"I wonder if I could have a meal in my room? I'd like to go to bed as soon as possible," she said, as porters carried their luggage into the lift.

"Certainly. Do whatever you wish," he said coolly. "We don't need to start out too early tomorrow. Will breakfast at eight-thirty suit you?"

Joanna nodded. She had a sudden wild impulse to rush down to the docks and catch the ferry back to Calais. But of course it was much too late to change her mind now.

Her bedroom was on the first floor and, as the lift purred

37

to a halt, Charles said, "I'll see you at breakfast, then. If there's anything you need, just phone down to the desk. The service is pretty good here."

"Yes, I will. Thank you. Goodnight," she said quietly.

His eyes were cold, and she fancied there was a flicker of derision in them, as if he guessed her cowardice and despised her for it.

"Goodnight," he said curtly, and, a moment later, the gates had closed and she was alone with her porter.

The bedroom to which he led her was comfortably appointed and agreeably warm. Spotless nylon glass-curtains shut out the dismal skyscape, and the sound of the wind was muted by the thick panes.

"Oh—I haven't any English money," Joanna exclaimed, in confusion, when the porter had set her cases on the chrome luggage rack and was hovering discreetly beside her. "I live in France, you see, and I haven't changed my francs yet."

"That's quite all right, miss," he said pleasantly. "Pretty rough in the Channel today, I should think. Never mind, the forecast says sun for tomorrow."

"Oh . . . good." Joanna was surprised. A French porter, even in a luxury hotel, would have looked very disdainful when no tip was forthcoming.

After a bath, and changed into pyjamas and a housecoat, she was brushing her hair and listening to the scatter of rain on the windows, when there was a light tap at the door. Thinking it was a waiter with her tray, she laid down her brush and hurried to open it. But it was Charles who stood in the corridor.

"I'm sorry if I disturbed you. I thought you would still be up," he apologised.

"I am. I'm waiting for my supper. Come in," she said, standing back.

He shook his head. "I only came to tell you that I've just put through a call to your grandmother."

"You told her you'd found me? What did she say?"

He looked at her with an expression she could not read. "She wants to speak to you."

38

"Now?"

"Yes. I've written down the number. It doesn't take long to get through." He handed her a slip of paper.

Joanna took it, her throat suddenly dry. "All right. I'll do it at once," she said unsteadily. "Do—do you want to listen to what I say?"

"I hardly think that will be necessary," he said. And turning, he walked away down the corridor and disappeared round a corner.

As she waited for the exchange to get the connection, Joanna found that her hands were trembling. At last, after a seemingly interminable interval, she heard the operator say, "Your number is ringing, caller."

Almost at once the distant receiver was lifted and, as clearly as if they were in adjoining rooms, she heard a voice say, "Joanna? Is that you, Joanna?"

"Yes, Mrs. Carlyon. It's Joanna speaking," she said huskily.

"Oh, my dearest child——" The voice quavered suddenly and broke off. There was an audible sniff and then, more steadily, the voice said, "Forgive me, my dear. So stupid of me to cry when I am so very happy. When Charles told me the news just now, I—I could hardly believe it."

Joanna swallowed. "I'm afraid it must have been a shock for you," she said in a low voice.

"Yes, it was, my dear. But such a very delightful one. You see, I was so afraid that, if we did find you, you wouldn't want to have anything to do with us. It would have been natural for you to feel full of hatred and resentment. But Charles tells me that you agreed to come at once. I'm so glad that you don't hate us, my poor child."

"No, of course I don't," Joanna said gently. "I only hope you won't be disappointed in me."

"I know we shall never be that," the voice said softly. "We're all looking forward to tomorrow. But there, I mustn't keep you chatting. Charles tells me you're very tired and are going to bed early. Sleep well, my dear, and, believe me, we welcome you most warmly. Goodnight, dear."

39

"Goodnight . . . Grandmother."

Joanna heard the click of the receiver being put back on the rest and quietly replaced her own. For a moment she sat very still on the edge of the bed, her lips quivering. And then, as the first slow tears began to course down her cheeks, she buried her face in her hands and wept for all the loneliness and pain of her long exile.

*　　　*　　　*

Charles was already seated at a table by the window when Joanna entered the hotel dining-room next morning. She had slept very well in the circumstances, and had been woken by a call from the porter's desk. Refreshed and full of new confidence, she had put on a navy linen suit over a white voile blouse. The suit had a pleated skirt and a collarless hip-banded jacket with a single huge pearl button at the neck. It was very simple and youthful—but also extremely *chic*. So there were interested glances as she followed the head waiter between the tables.

Charles had been reading a newspaper, but he rose as soon as he saw her and tossed the paper on to a spare chair.

"Would you care to try an English breakfast, or will you stick to rolls and coffee?" he asked, as she sat down.

"Oh, 'when in Rome . . .' I think," Joanna said, smiling.

"Does your self-discipline include a rigid diet?" he asked, when she had chosen grapefruit in preference to cereal or porridge.

"No. Fortunately I can eat as much as I like. Please—do go on reading your paper. I know it's the custom among Englishmen."

"And what is the custom in France?" he enquired drily. "Surely that excessive gallantry has some limits?"

"I don't know. I usually have breakfast alone," Joanna said lightly. "Oh—" remembering her difficulty with the porter the night before—"I wonder if you could let me have some English money. I have only francs and I couldn't tip the porter last night."

"Certainly. I should have remembered." He took some pound notes out of his wallet and a handful of silver from his pocket and put it by her plate.

Joanna thanked him and put it in her bag. As she looked

up, she caught a baleful stare from a stout matron at a near-by table.

"Something funny?" Charles asked.

Joanna concentrated on her grapefruit, trying not to laugh.

"Only that you've outraged our neighbour," she said quietly. "She obviously thinks I'm a shady character. I hope she won't complain to the management."

Charles shot a discreet glance at the other table and met a freezing glare.

"Sorry. That was rather tactless of me," he said.

"That reminds me," Joanna said thoughtfully. "Perhaps it would be better to cover up the fact that I work in cabaret. People always seem to think that night-club singers are devoid of morals, and I don't want to bring too much notoriety down on you."

"I fancy you'll attract a good deal of attention either way," he said with a faint smile.

"Oh? Why do you say that?" she asked seriously.

His glance travelled from her softly reddened mouth to her slim white hands with their immaculate rose-varnished nails. "We aren't used to Parisian elegance in our part of the world," he said mildly.

"Well, if you want me to, I'm quite willing to look dowdy," she said seriously.

His lips twitched. "No. As long as you don't appear in that spangled thing you were wearing the other night, I think you'll escape any serious censure," he said.

To her surprise, Joanna felt her colour rising. She had forgotten that on the night he had been to the cabaret she had been wearing that particular dress, the most *outré* of all her stage costumes. Suddenly, the realisation that he had seen her in it, both on stage and in the dressing-room, made her feel oddly uncomfortable.

"I suppose you were horrified," she said coolly.

"Not particularly." A gleam of laughter lit his eyes. "Compared with some of the dancers, your outfit was most decorous."

41

She fidgeted with her napkin. "I don't wear those things from choice. It's part of the job," she said awkwardly.

"You seem to take me for a very narrow-minded type," he said, pouring himself a second cup of tea.

"Not exactly. But it's one thing to see a girl in a . . . a scanty dress and not mind, but rather different when you find out she's a relative," Joanna stated.

"You forget. Our relationship is so distant as to be almost negligible," he observed.

An hour later, they began the last stage of the journey. The heavy mist of early morning was melting away and, as they left the town behind, a pale sun broke through the clouds.

Once on the fast arterial road to Maidstone, Charles let the car out, occasionally pointing out interesting landmarks but mostly saving his attention for the road. Soon they were on the outskirts of London, although, as Charles remarked, the environs of the Blackwall Tunnel were not a very prepossessing part of the great capital.

"Tell me, how did your father make a living?" he asked suddenly. "All this roving round the world can't have been done on air."

Joanna tensed slightly. She had been anticipating this question and had decided that, since she had a temperamental aversion to telling direct lies, she would have to parry it somehow. There were already enough cards against her without making matters worse, she had reflected.

But now, without knowing why, she had an impulse to tell him the truth.

"No, it wasn't," she agreed awkwardly. "At first, he had some kind of office job in Marseilles. But I suppose desk work must have been very dull and monotonous, and after a while he couldn't stand it."

"Why didn't he go back to painting?" Charles asked, when she paused for a moment.

"He did, for a time. We moved to Monaco and lived in a very cheap *pension*. But people weren't buying pictures then, and I think he had lost all ambition. Then one night he went to the casino and won a lot of money at baccarat."

42

She stopped again, remembering that long-ago summer night when she had woken up to find a great bunch of mimosa on her bedside table, and her father drinking champagne from a pink china toothbrush mug. He had let her taste it, the bubbles making her sneeze, and then he had sat on the side of the bed and pulled her hair and told her they were going to South America on the first boat out of Marseilles.

"We went to Rio," she said presently. "It took three weeks to get there and I wanted it to last for ever. After he'd put me to bed, Michael used to play cards with some businessmen. He was always playing after that—everywhere we went." She paused, fidgeting with the clasp of her bag. "I suppose I was about thirteen when I found out that he'd become a . . . a professional card-sharper," she said, very low. "I knew he played for money and nearly always won, but I didn't realise why."

"And this went on until his death?" Charles said, in an expressionless voice.

"Yes. That's how we lived—by cheating people," she said tonelessly. "And that's why we had to keep moving all the time. You see, after a while, the hotels and the shipping lines get to know you. You have to keep breaking fresh ground and f-finding new v-victims." Her voice shook and she turned her head away, not wanting him to see her face. "I'm sorry. I suppose I should have told you before. You would have changed your mind about bringing me to England, I expect. But you see, I never think of him as—as a crooked person. I didn't care what he did for a living. He was all I had. I—I would have loved him whatever he'd done."

"How did he die?" Charles asked quietly.

"He was knocked down by a car in the Champs Elysées," she said flatly. "His injuries were pretty bad, but they needn't have been fatal. He . . . he died because he didn't want to live any more."

"That was rather hard on you, wasn't it?" There was an edge of censure in his tone.

"It depends on how you look at it," she retorted coldly. "Maybe you can't imagine being so intensely in love with a woman that, without her, life would be meaningless. But

43

that's the way Michael felt about my mother. I—I was with him when he died. He thought I was Nina. It was the first time I'd seen him look really happy."

She had managed to keep her voice steady, but her eyes were smarting with tears and there was an aching lump in her throat. Fortunately Charles did not comment, and when he spoke again—to suggest that they should stop for lunch at a hotel a few miles ahead—she had composed herself.

Neither of them spoke much during the meal, and Joanna wondered if, in the light of her recent disclosures, Charles was regretting his decision to bring her to England.

As they started off again, she stifled a yawn. Presently, lulled by the murmur of the engine, she began to feel drowsy. She must have dozed as, when she opened her eyes, they had stopped at a filling station. Stretching, a little stiff, she saw that Charles was behind the car, chatting to the pump attendant.

"Only another ten miles," he said, sliding behind the wheel a few moments later. "What were you dreaming about? You've been talking in your sleep."

"Have I? I don't remember dreaming about anything," she answered, rather startled.

"Not to worry. It was all in French, so I didn't make much sense of it," he told her, with a gleam of amusement.

"You seemed to speak very good French the other night. Where did you pick it up? I thought most English people prided themselves on getting around by sign-language."

"They don't all have the incentive of a pretty foreign student living near them," he said carelessly. "Our next-door neighbours had a flirtatious French nursery help for a couple of years when I was still at the impressionable age. Unfortunately a lot of the phrases she taught me weren't much use for general conversation."

"I thought English boys weren't interested in girls until quite late in life," Joanna remarked.

"If they're stuck at a boarding school they don't get much chance to experiment. I went to the local grammar school."

44

"Even so I should have thought you'd have been interested in motor-bikes or sports, or something serious."

"I was," he said gravely. "But the best of motor-bikes looks better with a decorative brunette on the pillion."

There was a pause while Joanna tried to visualise him as a lanky teenager. But somehow it was impossible to imagine him in the throes of adolescence, his beard still little more than a darkening down, his features still stamped with immaturity.

"What happened to her?" she asked, presently.

"To Marie-Luce? Oh, she went home to Lyons. She'll be in her thirties by now and a staid and stout matron, I expect."

"She was older than you?"

"Of course. That was part of her attraction. Didn't you prefer older men when you were a dreamy sixteen-year-old?"

"I don't think I had any views on the subject. I didn't have dates at that age. Most of the people who go on expensive cruises are middle-aged or senile." And my dreams were of having a home and security, she added mentally.

"Weren't there any heart-throbs among the ship's officers?"

"Perhaps—I don't remember. Anyway, I wouldn't have interested them. I was still weighed down with puppy-fat and had bands on my teeth."

"What about your schooling?" he asked. "How was that fitted in?"

"It wasn't," she said baldly. "Michael couldn't afford to keep me at a boarding school, so I had to pick up what I could from books."

"You mean you had no formal education at all?"

"Not much. I did go to a day school in Marseilles for about a year when he was working for the foundry company, but not after we started travelling." She gave him a sideways glance. "I suppose that shocks you even more?"

"Have I looked shocked?" he enquired.

"No. But I expect you have been."

He smiled to himself. "Like all women, you assume too much," he said drily. "Why should I be shocked?"

"Well . . . it's scarcely a *usual* background, is it?

"Most unusual," he conceded. "But that doesn't make it scandalous. In fact, I think you must have rather a sheltered outlook to feel that your background is so shocking."

"I—sheltered?" Joanna exclaimed in amazement. "What on earth do you mean? I can't imagine anyone being *less* sheltered," she added, in a rather grim tone.

"Perhaps not—in the sense that you had to start fending for yourself at an earlier age than many girls and had no one to fall back on in an emergency," he agreed equably. "But just because your father made his living by card-sharping, and you haven't had the accepted form of education, I can't see any reason for your having to feel yourself a kind of social pariah."

Joanna gasped. "But I don't feel that at all!" she protested indignantly. "I never said I——"

He cut her short. "You may not admit it—even to yourself—but I think you do feel something of the kind," he said negligently. "In fact, you must be fairly self-conscious about your upbringing, or you wouldn't expect me to be scandalised."

Joanna counted five. "You've been reading a book on psychology, Cousin Charles," she said cuttingly. "But you're not as knowing as you think. Far from being ashamed of my circumstances, I'm rather proud of them. Personally, I feel there's something much more satisfying about making a go of life when the odds are against one. I should have been very bored if I'd merely *inherited* success."

But, as she might have guessed, it was too light a thrust to jar him into annoyance.

His only reaction was to give her an amused glance and a tolerant, "Let's leave it, for the time being, shall we? We'll be coming into Merefield in a moment."

Presently they entered a roundabout, and beyond it the countryside gave place to a prosperous-looking residential area with double gateways giving glimpses of large detached houses among carefully tended gardens. The centre of the town was crowded with parked cars and shoppers, and Joanna looked with interest at the attractive displays in the store windows and the striped awnings over the fruit and vegetable stalls in the central square. There was a rather hideous red brick Town Hall, an even uglier station and an enormous glass-and-concrete building which Charles said was the new technical college. Beyond this edifice, a broad street, punctuated at intervals by pedestrian crossings, led away from the shopping area. The buildings here were an incongruous mixture of modern flats, drab Victorian terraces and small private businesses. Then, turning right at a fork, they entered a modern housing estate.

To Joanna, growing more and more tense with every passing moment, the estate seemed vast. But at last the rows of almost identical houses came to an end and, crossing another main road, they turned up a quiet lane which had a high brick wall on one side of it. Presently the wall was broken by two tall stone pillars flanking a massive wrought-iron gate and, leaving the engine running, Charles swung out of his seat and went to open the gate.

Finding her compact, Joanna snapped it open and peered anxiously at her reflection in the little glass. She was hastily retouching her lips when Charles came back to the car and said, "Ready to make your entrance?"

She nodded, putting away her lipstick and holding tight to her bag to control the trembling of her hands.

The short gravelled drive was bordered by hedges of evergreen shrubs, and directly ahead of them stood the house. It was a solid Victorian structure with high gables and windows, with stained glass fanlights. Not an attractive house, nor one which looked homely and welcoming, Joanna thought nervously.

Charles drew the car up to the steps, and then got out again and went round to open the boot. Slowly, her knees feeling oddly weak, Joanna followed him.

"Ring the bell, will you? They can't have heard us coming," he said, lifting her cases out.

But before she could obey, the door opened and a tall grey-haired woman appeared on the threshold.

"Charles, my dear—how nice to have you back," she

said cordially, coming down the steps with both hands held out and a smile of welcome.

"Hello, Monica. All well?" He bent to kiss her cheek. Then, turning towards Joanna, he said, "Well, here she is— the prodigal granddaughter. Joanna, this is your aunt."

Joanna stepped forward, her hand held out.

"How do you do, Aunt Monica?" she said, with a diffident smile.

Her aunt looked at her with a cool appraising stare that missed no detail of her appearance.

"So you are Michael's daughter," she said slowly. "How do you do?"

But there was no warmth in the greeting and, as they followed her into the house, Joanna knew that even before they met, Monica Durrant had hated her.

CHAPTER THREE

"WHERE'S Grandmother? In the morning-room?" Charles asked, as they entered the hall.

"No, she's upstairs. I'm sorry to say that your trunk call last night had a rather upsetting effect on her," Mrs. Durrant replied, frowning slightly. "We were afraid she was going to have one of her attacks, so I thought it wiser to keep her in bed today. It would have been best if you had informed me first, Charles. I could have broken the news gently."

"Yes, I suppose I should have thought of that," Charles agreed concernedly. "She's all right, isn't she? There haven't been any changes while I've been away?"

"No, I think she's recovered now. But we had rather a bad night with her," the older woman said, with a sigh. She glanced at Joanna. "I don't know if Charles has explained to you, Miss Allen, but my mother suffers from heart trouble, so it's essential that she should not be agitated or distressed in any way. Please remember that when you see her."

"Yes, of course," Joanna said gravely. Then, hesitantly, "Won't you call me Joanna?"

"Why, yes, if you prefer it," her aunt replied. "Naturally in the circumstances it's a little difficult to realise that you are a member of the family." She opened a door and stood aside. "I'll ring for tea. You must be hungry after travelling all day."

"I dare say Joanna can last out for another half hour," Charles said. "Won't Grandmother be waiting for us? She's bound to have heard the car. I think we should go straight up to her."

"Certainly—if Joanna has no objection," Mrs. Durrant said.

"No, of course not. I'm looking forward to meeting her," Joanna said eagerly.

49

Her aunt flickered a strange and unreadable glance at her, and then turned back to the staircase and led the way. Had Joanna's mother been alive, she would have been in her late forties, and Joanna estimated that Monica Durrant was about forty-one or two. But for her grey hair—expertly cut and set, and tinted by a delicate lilac rinse—she could have passed for thirty-five. Her figure and legs were slim, and her face comparatively unlined. She was wearing a well-cut black skirt and an expensive crêpe-de-chine blouse with a triple strand of pearls at the neck and pearl-and-diamond clips in her ears. At first glance one would have described her as a gracious and attractive woman, but Joanna had already noticed that there was something curiously humourless about her face, and a hardness in the set of her mouth.

Mrs. Carlyon's bedroom was at the end of a long gloomy corridor which appeared to run the full length of the house. Tapping lightly on the door, her daughter opened it and walked in.

"They're here, Mother," she said, and beckoned her niece to enter.

The room was large and lofty, and Joanna had an impression of dark old-fashioned wallpaper and heavy mahogany furniture. Elaborate lace draperies shut out much of the light. But before she could take in any details, she found herself facing a massive Victorian bed, and in it, propped up by a mound of pillows, sat a white-haired old lady with a lacy Shetland shawl round her shoulders.

For a moment they gazed at each other in silence, and then, with a little cry, Mary Carlyon stretched out her withered hands and Joanna stepped forward and took them in her own young ones.

Afterwards, she could remember little of what they said in those first few minutes. She had no idea at what point Charles and her aunt retreated from the room. All she knew was that when, some time later, a maid brought in a tea tray, she was sitting on the side of the bed, and they were talking as easily as if they had known each other all her life.

"What a pretty child you are—and so very like your mother," Mrs. Carlyon said wistfully, as Joanna poured the tea. "No wonder Charles recognised you. Look, my dear,

I have her portrait over the fireplace. But for the hair-style and the dress, it might well be a picture of you."

Joanna turned and looked at the full-length painting which faced the bed. The few indifferent photographs which Michael had carried with him to the day of his death had shown her mother as a tall slim young woman with wide dark eyes and perfect teeth. But the painter of the portrait, more discerning than the lens of a cheap box camera, had captured more than Nina's colouring and grace. She had sat to him in a dress of willow green velvet against a background of mellow oak panelling, and such was the artist's skill that she seemed to glow with youth and gaiety and laughter, her lovely eyes shining with merriment.

"Her eyes were brown. Mine are hazel," Joanna said softly.

"Yes, you have Michael's eyes, but otherwise you are very like her. Even your voice is the same," her grandmother said, with a smile. "It's like having her back with me—as if we had never parted." Her voice trembled and she dabbed at her eyes with a handkerchief. "There now, I'm crying again. How silly of me," she said in a firmer tone. "You must be tired, dear. It's a long journey from Paris. I'll ring for Alice and you must have a rest and a bath before dinner. We have plenty of time to talk."

But before she could touch the bell pull beside the headboard there was a knock at the door and Charles looked in.

"Ah, Charles dear—just the person I wanted," Mrs. Carlyon said fondly. "Joanna must change and settle herself before we dine. She's having the north room. Show her the way, will you? And then you might ask Monica to come up. She insisted I should stay in bed today, but I am going to come down for dinner. I'm really perfectly well, and it makes so much extra work for Alice to have to bring trays up."

"Oh, please don't get up on my account," Joanna said anxiously. "Perhaps I could have a tray with you."

"No, no. I want to get up," her grandmother said firmly. "Monica likes to fuss me, but it's quite unnecessary. I'm as fit as a fiddle."

Charles grinned at her. "What's all this I hear about

your sneaking off for the afternoon while Monica was lunching with the Bradleys?" he asked teasingly.

"It was a lovely afternoon and I fancied a drive in the country, so I hired a car and had one," Mrs. Carlyon said with satisfaction. "I can't think why Monica had to make such a to-do about it. I might just as well die enjoying myself as shut up in here."

"I should be surprised if you didn't outlive the lot of us," Charles said drily. "I wish I could jaunt round the county on a fine day instead of being stuck at a desk."

Mrs. Carlyon chuckled. "You're not so hard done by, my lad," she said, with a shrewd glance. "I've no doubt you found more than the scenery to admire in Monaco. You must tell me about it some time. As much as is fit for me to hear, that is to say. Now run along, both of you. I'm going to get up."

In the corridor, Charles said, "How did it go?"

"Very well," Joanna answered, with a smile. "She's a delightful person. I can see why you're so fond of her."

He did not reply, and a moment later they reached the room which had been prepared for her. Like Mrs. Carlyon's, it was an old-fashioned apartment with a marble-topped washstand and high double bed.

"The bathroom is next door. Dinner's at seven. You'll hear the gong," Charles said.

"Are you going to your own house now?" she asked.

"No, I'm just going to take my luggage back and collect the mail and then I shall come back here for the evening," he said. "Or would you rather I left you to cope alone?"

"Oh, no! I'd be glad for you to stay," she said quickly. Then, on impulse: "Why does my aunt dislike me, Charles? She was very polite, but I could tell she wasn't pleased to see me."

He jingled the coins in his pocket, glancing about the room. "You must have imagined it. Why should she dislike you?" he said casually. "As she said, it's difficult to realise you're a member of the family. There's bound to be a certain amount of reserve to overcome. They've put out towels and so forth, haven't they? Ah, yes. Well, I'll be off. See you later."

52

"Yes. Thank you," Joanna said quietly.

But when he had closed the door, his receding footsteps muffled by the thick carpets, she remained in the centre of the room, absently twisting her bracelet, a puzzled frown contracting her brows.

Presently, shrugging aside the enigma of her aunt's hostility, she began to unpack, hanging her suits and dresses in the large camphor-smelling wardrobe, and arranging her smaller possessions neatly in the dressing-table drawers.

The bathroom proved to be as old-fashioned as the rest of the house, with green bead curtains screening the lower half of the window, a vast airing cupboard, and a lavatory enclosed in a throne of highly polished oak. However, the plumbing was evidently modern, as the hot tap gave forth a strong jet of almost boiling water.

Back in her room, Joanna selected a semi-formal long dress of mint green wild silk. A skein of faceted crystals filled the modest décolletage, and she pinned up her hair to show the matching ear-clips.

She was ready by half-past six, and after looking out at the garden for some minutes she decided to go downstairs. The taps were running in the bathroom as she passed the door and she wondered which member of the household was the occupant. One of her cousins perhaps. She wondered if they would follow their mother's lead and receive her with the same cold courtesy.

The hall was deserted as she walked down the stairs, but as she reached the bottom the front door was flung open and a tall fair-haired young man rushed in and tossed a briefcase on to an oak rug chest. Turning towards the stairs, he saw her and stopped short, a look of rather comical astonishment on his face.

"Good lord! Are *you* Cousin Joanna?" he asked, after a moment.

Joanna smiled, wondering what he had expected her to be like, since it was plain that the reality amazed him.

"That's right," she said pleasantly. "And you're Neal, I presume?"

He nodded, his glance travelling slowly from the crown of her head to the toes of her pearl grey shoes. "Well, you are a surprise!" he said emphatically. "Here were we, waiting to be kind to little Orphan Annie, and what do we find? A gorgeous redhead straight out of a fashion magazine!"

It was said too frankly to be in any way offensive, and Joanna laughed and held out her hand. "Thank you," she said demurely. "But I think Merefield must be rather behind the times if this dress looks at all striking. It wouldn't rate a second glance in Paris, I'm afraid."

His handshake was warm and firm and, now that he had recovered from his amazement, his expression was as friendly as his mother's had been guarded.

"You'd rate a second glance anywhere," he said appreciatively. "Are they all busy changing? Come and have a drink and let me get used to you." And taking her arm, he steered her round a corner and into a handsome drawing-room which overlooked a rose garden.

"What'll you have? A sherry—or something stronger?" he asked, going over to a cabinet near the fireplace.

"A sherry would be lovely," Joanna said, studying him with interest.

He was tall—although not as tall as Charles—and slimly built, with a thin rather Puckish face and hazel eyes. As he poured their drinks, she noticed that he had beautiful hands with long supple fingers and very clean nails.

"What time did you get here? Have you met all the others?" he asked, filling two glasses and bringing them across to her.

"Not your sisters. I think they were out when we arrived," she said, sitting down on a large brocaded sofa.

Neal pulled up a small table and sat down beside her. "Cigarette?" he asked, offering her his case.

"No, thank you. I don't smoke."

He grinned. "Pity. You're the type to brandish one of those foot-long diamond-studded holders. I'm afraid poor old Vanessa is going to feel the draught a bit from now on."

"Your sister? What do you mean?" Joanna asked, puzzled.

Neal laughed. "Up to today Vanessa's been the belle of the ball around here," he explained. "Not that there's a great deal of competition in this neck of the woods. But I have a feeling that the lads of the village are going to find her a trifle insipid now you're around."

Joanna sipped the sherry. "I dare say you mean that as a compliment, but it's not a very nice thing to say about your sister," she said with a level glance.

He shrugged. "I'm not a very nice person, dear cousin. In fact—as our worthy Charles has probably warned you— I'm the second blackest sheep in the family."

"The second? Who is the first?" she asked.

He slanted a speculative glance at her. "Your father, of course," he said drily.

Joanna wondered how he expected her to react. "What was your particular crime?" she enquired mildly.

"Oh, nothing specific. I just don't match up to the great Carlyon tradition. Life is real, life is earnest—all that kind of thing," he said negligently.

Before Joanna could reply, there were footsteps outside the door and two girls came in.

Neal stood up. "My sisters, Cousin Joanna," he said. "Come and make polite conversation, you two. I'd better go and clean up before the Elders come down." And with a smile at Joanna, and a quizzical glance at his sisters, he downed his drink and left the room.

For some seconds after his departure, there was a slightly awkward pause, and then the younger of the girls moved forward and said with engaging frankness, "I must say you're not a bit what we expected—is she, Van?"

Joanna laughed. "What did you expect?" she asked.

Cathy Carlyon sat down in a chair opposite her. "I don't know really. Someone rather shabby and trodden-on, I suppose," she said reflectively.

"Oh, Cathy, what rubbish you always talk," her sister said, looking embarrassed. "Did you have a good journey, Miss Allen?"

"Yes, thank you. Very good," Joanna responded politely.

Vanessa went to the cabinet and poured herself a glass

55

of sherry. She was plainly ill at ease, and Joanna wondered if she was always on edge with strangers or if, like her mother, she was hostile and wary.

Although both sisters had fair hair and fresh complexions, they were not particularly alike. Vanessa was tall and statuesque with a straight nose and firmly rounded chin. Cathy was small and coltish with a scatter of freckles on her forehead and short snub nose. Vanessa wore her hair in a glossy long bob, but the younger girl's hair was cropped close to her head and not very tidy.

"Where's Charles? Has he gone home?" Cathy enquired.

"Only to leave his luggage. He's coming back," Joanna told her.

"Oh, good. I wonder if he's brought us any presents?" Cathy said hopefully. "How do you get on with him? Has he been nice to you?"

"Yes, very nice. Is there any reason why he shouldn't have been?" Joanna asked.

"Oh, no—but he can be awfully sarcastic sometimes," Cathy said candidly. "I've known people to be scared to death of him. He has a funny way of looking at you—as if he knew what you were thinking."

"It's not very polite to discuss people behind their backs, Cathy," Vanessa said abruptly. "Will you have another drink, Miss Allen?"

Joanna shook her head. "No, thank you. I haven't finished this one yet."

"Can we call you Joanna?" Cathy asked. "It seems so silly to call you 'Miss Allen' when you're a relation."

Joanna smiled at her. "Yes, do," she said warmly.

"What a lovely dress," Cathy said, eyeing it admiringly. "The clothes shops in Merefield are deadly. Full of serviceable tweeds and deadly dull twin sets. Absolute death after Paris, I should think."

"Well, I expect tweeds and sweaters are the best choice in the provinces," Joanna said. "The Frenchwoman's elegance is really rather a myth, you know. It's only in Paris or Cannes that people dress to kill. As a matter of fact, I made this myself."

56

"Did you honestly? Gosh, how clever. I thought it was a model," Cathy said, impressed. "I wish I could sew properly. I made this skirt, but there's something wrong with the hem." She jumped up to demonstrate that the hang of her full blue skirt was faulty.

"The cut is all right. You need a lining—or a waist petticoat," Joanna suggested. "Have you got one? If not, you can borrow one of mine."

"Can I really? That's awfully decent of you," Cathy said, looking surprised. "Vanessa hates lending things, don't you, Van?"

"If you tried to plan your clothes instead of buying the first thing that catches your eye, you wouldn't need to borrow," her sister said repressively. "Don't let her start cadging, Miss Allen . . . Joanna. She's fearfully clumsy—always spilling things down herself or tearing huge rents."

"I'm *not*," Cathy protested indignantly. "It wasn't my fault that Bill Harris shot his coffee all over that red blouse of yours. Anyway, I had it cleaned, so you needn't keep on about it so."

"Yes, but you didn't ask if you could wear it, did you?" Vanessa said coldly.

Cathy flushed and shot an anxious glance at Joanna, obviously resenting this revelation of her imperfections before a stranger. Fortunately, before she could snap back a retort, the door opened again and Charles strolled in.

Immediately, both girls forgot their grievances. Cathy dashed forward with an exclamation of delight, and Vanessa's censorious expression gave place to a smile of pleasure.

"Charles! How heavenly to have you back," Cathy cried eagerly, flinging her arms round his neck and planting an uninhibited kiss on his lean brown cheek. "What have you brought us?" she demanded. "Some naughty French scanties, or a whacking great bottle of scent?"

Charles extricated himself from her bear-like embrace and ruffled her hair. "What makes you think I've brought you anything?" he asked, with an indulgent grin. "Hello, Vanessa."

He took the older girl's hands in his and smiled down at

her. Watching them, Joanna saw a delicate flush suffuse her cousin's cheeks.

"Oh, don't be such a sadist, Charles. I know you've got *something* up your sleeve," Cathy broke in impatiently.

"Not up my sleeve, little one. On the hall table," Charles said, dropping into a chair. "I dare say you don't deserve it, but I suppose you'd better have it since I've squandered some of my francs on you."

Cathy rushed out of the room, and, lighting a cigarette, Charles looked across at Joanna.

"There's only Neal to meet now," he said. "I expect he'll be late. He usually is."

"She's already met him," Vanessa said quickly. "Did you have a good time, Charles? You're wonderfully sun-tanned."

Before he could reply Cathy burst back again, clutching two parcels. One she tossed to her sister, the other she began hurriedly to unfasten.

"Ooh—trousers! Just what I want!" she exclaimed rapturously, holding up a pair of vivid harlequin beach pants with a matching tunic. "Hope they fit. What gorgeous colours. This'll knock their eyes out at the Country Club. Thanks a million, Charles."

Charles submitted to another boisterous hug and allowed her to settle on the side of his chair, an arm round his shoulders. His gift to Vanessa proved to be a blouse of handtucked white chiffon with a demure Peter Pan collar. It was the kind of thing which rich American tourists bought at exclusive little *boutiques,* and Joanna could guess how much it had cost. She wondered if he was always generous, or if he had a special affection for the elder sister. Certainly his taste was impeccable. The blouse was a perfect choice for Vanessa's fresh white-and-gold beauty.

"Thank you, Charles. It's lovely," the girl said quietly. "I'll wear it tonight. I shan't be a moment."

As she left the room, her mother and grandmother entered, the old lady leaning on her daughter's arm.

"Ah, there you are, my dears," she said fondly. "What have you got there, Cathy? It looks very gay."

"Charles has bought me a beach suit, Gran. Do you like it?"

"It's certainly very striking," Mrs. Carlyon said, with a twinkle. "There'll be no danger of losing sight of you. Ah, there's the gong. Let's go in, shall we? Our two travellers must be hungry."

Neal was waiting for them at the dining-room door and, while Charles drew out chairs for the two older women, he saw Joanna seated and took the place next to her. A few minutes, later, while the maid was serving the soup, Vanessa reappeared in the new blouse.

"What a charming blouse, dear. Most becoming," Mrs. Carlyon said approvingly. "And what have you brought for Monica and me, Charles? Or are we past the age for these exciting presents?"

"I'll give you yours after dinner, Grandmother. You know what Cathy is. She couldn't wait," he said, smiling. "How have things been going at the factory, Neal? Smoothly, I hope."

"I think so. They generally do," Neal said carelessly. He turned to Joanna. "How did Charles come across you?" he asked.

Joanna hesitated and, before she could answer, Charles said, "In a night club. I thought I recognised her, and that bracelet confirmed it."

"A night club, eh?" Neal said, looking interested. "Did you lead a very gay life in Paris, Joanna?"

"No, not really," she said cautiously. "Do you know Paris?"

"I spent a week there once. I wouldn't say I know it," he replied. "What night club? Not the Folies Bergère, I hope." He shot an amused glance at Charles.

"I wish there was a night club in Merefield," Cathy remarked, with a sigh. "It's deadly here, Joanna. Everyone goes to bed about ten."

"You're too young for night clubs anyway," Vanessa observed. "I should think they're rather nasty places."

"You would," her brother said derisively. "We can't all be fresh air fanatics."

"Do you ride, my dear?" Mrs. Carlyon asked Joanna. "Vanessa is a very keen horsewoman."

"No, I'm afraid I don't. I've never had time for any sports."

"Thank God for that," Neal said succinctly. "Athletic women are an abomination."

"No more abominable than third-rate artists who think they're geniuses," Vanessa said cuttingly.

Mrs. Carlyon forestalled any rejoinder. "Really, my dears, one would think you were still in the nursery," she said, in gentle reproach. "Poor Joanna will imagine we all hate each other if you squabble over trifles. Now, Charles dear, tell us about your holiday before you found Joanna. Was the weather good?"

When the meal was over, they adjourned to the drawing-room and Charles took the opportunity to draw Joanna aside for a moment and say quietly, "I think you'll have to tell the old lady the truth. How much the others are told must depend on her. She will probably go to bed soon and want you to talk to her, so you may well tell her at once and then it will be done with."

Joanna nodded and they drew apart. But, catching Vanessa's eye, she saw that her cousin had observed the brief exchange and was watching her with unmistakable enmity. So she's on her mother's side, Joanna thought unhappily. Three are for me, and three against me. At least, I suppose Charles is against me—or he would be if he didn't want to make Mrs. Carlyon happy. Oh well, it could be worse.

As Charles had forecast, Mrs. Carlyon retired early and asked Joanna to visit her when she was in bed.

"My dear, I couldn't help noticing your slightest hesitation when Neal asked about your meeting with Charles," she said, when they were alone. "Please don't feel that, in coming here, you are under an obligation to tell me anything which you would prefer to remain private. You owe me nothing, child: but I can never repair the harm I have done you."

"But you've done me no harm, Grandmother," Joanna protested.

"Oh yes, dear child, a great wrong," Mrs. Carlyon said

sadly. "I should never have allowed your grandfather to overrule me. I should have been stronger. Perhaps if I tell you what began it, you will find it easier to forgive me."

"There's nothing to forgive," Joanna said gently. "It wasn't your fault that Grandfather disliked my father. And he was your husband. Naturally, your first loyalty was to him."

A strange sad smile twisted the old lady's mouth. "No; that was why John was such a hard man," she said quietly. "You see, my first loyalty was to someone else—someone he never knew." And then, slowly and painfully, she told Joanna of the bitter and needless jealousy which had marred the lives of three generations.

"You may find it hard to believe, but I was thought very pretty as a girl," she began with a wry smile. "My hair was golden then, and I used to put slices of cucumber on my face to improve my complexion. We had no cosmetics with which to enhance Nature in those days—or at least such things were never used by respectable women. So, because the plain girls had so few means of improving themselves, a naturally pretty face was a much greater asset than it is today. You have to remember that there were no film stars to set a standard of beauty. I imagine that, had I been born fifty years later, no one would have given me a second glance. But, as things were then, I was something of a belle—and very vain and frivolous into the bargain."

She paused for a moment, and Joanna pressed her hand and said gently, "I'm sure you were lovely, Grandmother—and not a bit vain."

Mrs. Carlyon shook her head regretfully. "I had a great many *beaux*," she went on, "and one of them was your grandfather. He was ten years older than I, and I thought him rather pompous and dull—although I was secretly flattered by his attentions. Because our families encouraged the match and because he was the most eligible of my admirers, I accepted his proposal. I'm afraid I was rather mercenary. I liked the idea of being a married woman with my own establishment and a carriage and a staff of servants. I dreamed of playing hostess and holding elegant 'at homes' and soirées. The responsibilities of marriage never occurred to me."

She fell silent for a time, and Joanna saw her lips compress with remembered pain.

"Within a month of the announcement of our engagement, I met David Lovell," the old lady continued. "All at once I saw how foolish I had been to promise myself to John. For a while I tried to suppress my feelings for David, but each time we met I fell more deeply in love with him—and I knew that he loved me too. Then, after several weeks of trying to hide what had happened to me, we met at a ball. I knew it was wrong, but I went for a stroll in the garden with him. I was wearing a white satin dress with garlands of pale green gauze on the skirt and white camellias in my hair. The garden was bathed in moonlight and the musicians were playing a waltz. As we walked towards the shadow of an arbour, I knew I ought to make some excuse to go back—but I didn't. If only I had."

Her voice quivered and she pressed a handkerchief to her lips for a moment.

"Please, Grandmother—don't go on if it distresses you," Joanna said anxiously.

Mrs. Carlyon sniffed and braced her frail shoulders. "No, no—I want to tell you," she insisted. "It's silly of me to be so sentimental about it." Then, quickly dabbing her eyes and tucking the handkerchief away, she went on in a firmer tone, "Once David had declared his feelings, I knew I could never put up the pretence any longer. I told John the truth. I was not particularly surprised when he took it quite calmly, as I assumed that his affection for me was no deeper than mine for him, and I thought he would soon find someone else. My parents were very angry with me and might have refused to countenance an engagement to David, but the first world war was imminent and overshadowed all minor catastrophes." She reached out a hand and touched Joanna's cheek, her face softening with affection.

"I was lucky to be young before the world went mad," she said softly. "Our youthful troubles seem very trivial compared with the shadows that have fallen on your young lives. However, I don't want to bore you with my ramblings. I must keep to the point. Just pour me a little water, will you, dear?"

Joanna did so, and watched the veined old hand raise the

cut glass tumbler. Looking at the stiff fingers, the withered skin, she had a sudden sharp awareness of the transience of youth, of how quickly the years flew by. So few years, so little time in which to grasp all the richness and variety life had to offer. Had she been wasting that time? Had ambition and the subconscious craving for security made her blind to the other things?

A little afraid of thoughts that were too introspective, she was relieved when her grandmother began to speak again. Although she had come to the saddest part of her story, Mrs. Carlyon did not falter as she described the first terrible months of that first "great" war, and the personal agony of mind which it had brought to her. For David Lovell had been among the first casualties, while John Carlyon had come through the four long years of blood-shed with one minor wound and a brilliant record of gallantry.

Since no one can grieve for ever, by the time the Armistice came Mary Carlyon no longer wept for her lost love. But the war years had changed her from a charming social butterfly into a more thoughtful and understanding young woman. In 1920, John Carlyon proposed to her for the second time and, with a new appreciation of his worth, she accepted.

Within weeks of their marriage, Mary found that it was not only liking and respect which she felt for him. And if this second love was quieter and less romantic than her brief idyll with David, it was no less precious. Grateful for another chance of happiness, she never guessed that John was secretly tormented by thoughts of the past. Only gradually did it dawn on her that her husband's strange moods of coldness and withdrawal were prompted by a deep-rooted and seemingly incurable jealousy of the boy who had so briefly supplanted him. The violence of this jealousy was to mar their whole life together.

As their first child, Nina, grew up, Mary was troubled by the obsessive quality of her father's devotion to her. Nina had always been his favourite, but while indulging her every whim he seemed to resent her friendships with other young people—particularly young men. Mary was afraid that when Nina fell in love, her father's jealousy would find a new focus.

The crisis, when it came, was even worse than she had feared. Nina returned from a visit to friends in London with an attentive escort. As soon as they stepped out of the taxi it was obvious that they were wildly in love. What was even worse, she was already wearing an engagement ring.

Perhaps if Michael Allen had been a sober-minded young businessman, John Carlyon might eventually have accepted him. But Michael was not only an impecunious artist, but thirty-one to Nina's seventeen. As soon as he learned of the engagement, John Carlyon flew into a towering rage and ordered his prospective son-in-law out of the house. Michael left—and the next day Nina followed him. A fortnight later she wrote to her mother from Paris. She was married —although it probably wasn't legal, she added unconcernedly—and deliriously happy. She felt sure Daddy would soon get over his anger and then they would come and see them. Perhaps by that time she would be having a baby. Paris was heaven. Michael was an angel to her.

When Mary nerved herself to show the letter to John, she braced herself for another outburst. With an icy calm that was even more terrifying than his fury, he read the letter and tore it into pieces. Nina's portrait was taken down, all her possessions destroyed. It was as though she had never existed. And, as if Nina's default had killed all that was good in him, Mary had to watch her husband growing daily more harsh and cold. He broke her heart, but she never ceased to love him.

When, at last, the tired old voice lapsed into silence, Joanna's eyes were bright with tears.

"Don't cry, child," Mrs. Carlyon said gently. "It's no use regretting what is past. We can never retrieve our mistakes—only learn from them." She raised a hand and touched the girl's cheek. "She wrote to me, you know," she said with a smile. "Your grandfather never knew, but I had several letters from her. And then, one day, there was a letter from Michael, and that was the last I heard until after your grandfather's death. Poor child, how terrible for you to be left so alone in the world. If only we could have found you sooner."

"It wasn't really so terrible, Grandmother," Joanna said

reassuringly. "You needn't have worried about me. I managed."

And omitting as much as she could of the darker side, she told her grandmother most of what had happened in the years since her father's death. Rather surprisingly, Mrs. Carlyon was not at all shocked to learn how she earned her living and saw no reason why the other members of the family should not be told.

"There's nothing at all disreputable about working in a cabaret, dear," she said reasonably. "I'm delighted to hear that you've been so successful. You must give us a private performance one evening. I'm sure the children will be most excited when they learn you're quite a famous person."

"Not yet, but I hope to be one day," Joanna said, laughing. "You know, it seems——"

She broke off as the door opened and her aunt came in.

"It's getting late, Mother. Time you were asleep," Mrs. Durrant said, bringing a glass of hot milk to the bedside. "Too much talking tires her," she added to Joanna.

"Oh, yes . . . well, I'll say goodnight, then, Grandmother," Joanna said hurriedly. "I'm sorry if I've stayed too long."

"Nonsense, my dear, of course you haven't," Mrs. Carlyon assured her. "Monica likes to pamper me, but I'm a great deal hardier than she thinks. However, I expect you're tired. Now that we've had our little talk I feel we really know each other. Goodnight, dear. Sweet dreams."

"Goodnight, Grandmother." Joanna bent to kiss the old lady's cheek, and then, with a murmured goodnight to her aunt, she left the room.

*   *   *

She was woken up next morning by the drone of a motor mower below her window, and, blinking at the clock, she saw with dismay that it was past ten. Scrambling out of bed, she snatched up her housecoat and was tying the sash when there was a tap at the door and the maid entered.

"Oh, you're up, miss. I just looked in to see if you'd woken yet. I'll bring your tray up straight away," she said pleasantly.

"Oh, no, please! I'll come downstairs. I'd no idea it was so late," Joanna said apologetically.

"That's all right, miss. Madam left instructions that you weren't to be disturbed until you woke. Your tray's all ready. It's no trouble."

"Are you sure?" Joanna asked diffidently. "I don't want to be a nuisance. You see, I usually work late at night and don't get up till mid-morning. I shall need an alarm clock to help me break the habit."

The woman assured her again that it was no trouble and presently she returned with a tray and set it on a table by the window.

"I hope you can eat grapefruit, miss. If not, just leave it. I'll get to know your preference by and by," she said, in a friendly tone. "There's bacon and eggs under the cover."

Joanna looked at the tray which was laden with toast and marmalade and fresh fruit.

"I usually have coffee and a roll. This will last me all day," she said, smiling. "Thank you very much . . . Alice, isn't it?"

"Yes, miss. Alice Burrows. Madam said I was to tell you that she and Miss Vanessa have gone shopping. They won't be back till lunch. Mrs. Carlyon's in the morning-room, reading the papers."

"Oh, thank you. Well, I'll try to eat this enormous breakfast, and then I'll dress and go down to Grandmother," Joanna said with a smile.

It was nearly eleven when she carried the tray downstairs and found her way to the kitchen. Alice was not about, so she left it on the dresser and returned to the hall, wondering which door led into the morning-room. As she hesitated, a car drew up to the house and a moment later Charles come in.

"Good morning," he said. "Where are the others?"

Joanna told him. He was wearing a grey linen shirt and whipcord slacks, and the casual, rather shabby garments made him look younger and a little less autocratic.

"Aren't you back at work today?" she asked, surprised.

66

"I looked in earlier, but I'm not back officially until next week," he said casually. "Morning, Alice. Any coffee going?"

The maid, coming out of the drawing-room, stopped. "Yes, Mr. Charles. Shall I bring it into the morning-room? Mrs. Carlyon will be having her chocolate in a moment."

"Yes, please." Charles turned to Joanna. "This way," he said, slipping a hand under her elbow.

It was the briefest and most casual of gestures, but for the few seconds that his cool dry fingers touched her arm, she experienced a most curious sensation—like a current running through her.

Mrs. Carlyon was deep in the *Daily Telegraph* and it was some seconds before she became aware of them.

"Good morning, dear. Good morning, Charles. Are you lunching with us?" she enquired.

"If I may," he said with a smile. "I thought Vanessa might like a game of tennis this afternoon. I gather it hasn't rained lately, so the court should be reasonably sound."

"I'm sure she'll be delighted. She was trying to persuade Neal to play with her the other evening, but he wanted to go out," Mrs. Carlyon said. "How did you sleep, Joanna?"

"Much too well. I was horified when I found how late it was," Joanna said. "Does Cathy come home for lunch, or does she have it at school?"

"At school," her grandmother said. "You know, Charles, I'm rather worried about Cathy. Monica says there's nothing the matter with her, but she's been very moody lately, not a bit like her normal self. I wonder if she's got into some scrape. I wish you'd try and find out. She's so fond of you that she might feel encouraged to confide something she wouldn't admit to her mother."

"All right. I'll have a chat with her," he agreed. "I dare say it's nothing serious. She's probably in love with the boy next door or something like that."

"Not the boy next door. He's a *most* unprepossessing youth," Mrs. Carlyon said, chuckling. "But it might well be the new dentist. I'm told he's very good-looking and she's been having several fillings done lately."

At this point Alice came in with the coffee and a cup of chocolate for her employer.

"It was ever so good of you to bring your tray down, Miss Joanna," she said. "Will you be here to lunch, Mr. Charles?"

"Yes, please, Alice. By the way, is the boiler running properly now?"

"Yes, it's been going a treat since you had the men to look at it. The fridge don't seem too good, though. It keeps making a funny noise, a kind of clanking. I don't know what's come over it," Alice said perplexedly.

"I'll come and have a look," Charles said, getting up.

When he had left the room, Mrs. Carlyon said, "I don't know how we should manage without Charles. He's such a capable boy. He looks after everything for us, and is a tower of strength in any emergency."

"I should think he would be," Joanna said carefully. "Are his parents dead?"

"Yes, they were killed in a car when he was quite a child. Your grandfather took him into the factory when he left school and now, of course, he's chairman of the board and takes a very active part in the management."

"Isn't he rather young for such a position?" Joanna suggested.

"Exceptionally young," her grandmother agreed. "But then he's exceptionally able."

"Grandmother, I wonder if I could make a telephone call to Paris some time today," Joanna asked presently. "My agent will want to know where I am, and there wasn't time to give him this address before I left. I could write, but I'd rather like to speak to him. Naturally, I'll pay you whatever it costs."

"Of course you may telephone him, dear. Why not book the call now, in case there is some delay. As soon as Charles comes back he can show you the study. There is an extension on the desk and you can speak in private. But tell me, if you were singing in a cabaret, how is it that you were able to come home with Charles immediately?"

Joanna explained that her contract had run out and

that the Cordiale always closed down for six weeks in the summer while the décor was changed.

"There are very few tourists in Paris in August, you see. It's generally too hot and dusty for comfortable sightseeing," she added. "If Charles hadn't arrived on the scene, I was planning to have a quiet holiday in Brittany."

"I see. And what are your plans for——?" her grandmother began. But before she could finish the question, Charles came back and she postponed her enquiry to ask him to show Joanna the study. "She wants to telephone a friend in Paris," she explained to him.

"I doubt if you'll get through straight away," Charles remarked, when they were in a small book-lined room at the back of the house. He rattled up the slats of some oldfashioned wooden blinds which had been filtering the sunlight. "Incidentally, how did the boy-friend react when you told him you were shooting off to England?"

Joanna sat down in the heavy swivel chair behind the writing-desk and reached for the telephone receiver. "The boy-friend?" she repeated blankly. There had been so much to occupy her mind in the past forty-eight hours that, for the moment, she had completely forgotten Yves's existence.

Charles leaned against the corner of the desk, hands in pockets, his expression faintly sardonic.

"Evidently those opulent-looking ear-rings didn't make the impression he hoped they would," he said drily. "Or is he the 'friend' you are so anxious to ring?"

"I'm ringing my agent," Joanna retorted coolly. "He doesn't know where I am, and we have some bookings to discuss."

Charles straightened. "Business before pleasure . . . mm? All the same, I should give the boy-friend a tinkle, if I were you. He may not qualify for that gilt-edged marriage you're planning, but sapphires are worth some acknowledgment." Before she had time to retaliate, he had left the room.

Joanna glared after him for a moment, then shrugged and lifted the receiver. The operators told her there would be only a few minutes' delay on a call to Paris, so she stayed where she was.

Now that Charles had reminded her of it, she had to

69

decide what to do with Yves's present. True, a gift of sapphires meant no more to Yves than some pretty costume trinket to a man who worked for his living. All the same, she didn't feel comfortable about keeping the ear-rings. Yet, if she returned them, she might hurt him even more than she had done already.

She was still debating the problem when the operator called her back. A few moments later she was connected to Gustave's office. The agent was not on the premises, but his secretary took down the Merefield address and telephone number, and it was oddly comforting to hear a staccato French voice. Joanna was tempted to call the Dinards, but guessed that they would be so flustered by a cross-Channel conversation that they would never take in her explanation.

Returning to the morning-room, she ignored Charles's interrogative glance and hastily took an interest in the embroidery on Mrs. Carlyon's tambour. Presently her aunt and Vanessa returned, and there was no further opportunity for him to attempt to ruffle her. But once or twice while they were all having lunch together, she was aware of his glance resting on her and was made oddly restive and self-conscious by it.

After lunch Mrs. Carlyon went upstairs to rest, and Joanna asked her aunt if she might use their ironing board to press some of her dresses.

"I hope my arrival hasn't made a great deal of extra work," she said apologetically, as Mrs. Durrant showed her the small first-floor ironing-room.

"Not at all. I'm afraid you'll find it very quiet here, but perhaps you won't mind that for a fortnight," her aunt said coolly. "Excuse me. I have some things to attend to."

Joanna fetched her clothes and plugged in the iron. There was no sign of her aunt warming towards her. Indeed, the rather pointed remark about the duration of her niece's visit suggested that closer acquaintance had increased Mrs. Durrant's animosity.

Waiting for the iron to warm up, Joanna leaned against the window. It overlooked the hard tennis court at the back of the house, and as she stood there, Charles and Vanessa came into view. Both had changed into tennis kit, and Vanessa's short princess style tunic enhanced her generously proportioned figure. As a schoolgirl she had probably been plump if not buxom, but now, her puppy fat fined down, she was what people called "a handsome figure of a girl" and probably more attractive to masculine eyes than a more willowy type. Watching them unlash the tarpaulin cover on the net, Joanna thought how well they looked together. Charles, tall and dark and lithe, and Vanessa, so fair and limber and healthy-looking.

Turning back to the ironing board, she began to press a skirt. It seemed much more than two days since she had left Paris, and suddenly she felt a pang of something close to homesickness for her room above the Café Bernadine and for the sounds and scents of the *quartier*.

From below the window came the hollow clop-clop of ball hitting racquet, and unconsciously Joanna frowned. She slipped the skirt back on its hanger and took down an Italian silk shirt, carefully adjusting the temperature control to suit the material.

"You're out of condition. It's all that lazing about on the Riviera!"

The clear, rather high-pitched voice drifted upwards and there was an answering laugh from the far end of the court, followed by the crack of a powerful service.

Joanna twitched impatiently at a fold of the shirt and applied the iron. What was the matter with her? Why should the sounds of the game make her feel shut out—an unwanted interloper in a circle which had been complete before she came, and would still be so when she had gone?

The last dress pressed, she went back to her room and put the clothes away. There were some books on a shelf near the fireplace. She took a couple, slipped off her blouse and skirt, and lay down to read off her unreasonable mood.

Some time later there was a soft scratch at the door, and, in answer to her "Come in," Cathy's head appeared.

"Oh, sorry. Were you asleep?"

"No. Just being lazy. Come and talk to me," Joanna said, sitting up.

Cathy advanced into the bedroom. She was wearing her school uniform and looked gawky and rather wan.

"Phew, what a foul day! I'm so sick of school I could scream. Thank heavens we break up on Friday," she said,

71

hitching herself on to the end of the bed. Then, her eyes brightening: "I say, what super undies. You must have a marvellous job to afford all your lovely clothes. What do you do, Joanna?"

Joanna told her, wondering what her reaction would be.

"No! Not really!" Cathy exclaimed incredulously. "Oh, *what* a stroke of luck. Absolutely heaven-sent! You're just the person I need!"

"What do you mean?" Joanna asked, puzzled.

"Why, to back me up, of course, when I drop my bombshell," her cousin said excitedly. "Look, swear you won't tell—at least, not till the right moment."

"No, I won't tell, if it's a secret."

Cathy settled herself more comfortably, kicking off her shoes and then clasping her arms round her knees. "You know I leave school at Christmas," she began. "Well, Ma and Vanessa want me to go to a secretarial college. I'm not a bit brainy, you see, so there's no point in going on to university, or anything like that."

"So?" Joanna prompted.

"I don't want to be a secretary," Cathy said flatly. "I'm not even sure that I *could* be one. I'd probably end up as a pretty hopeless copy typist in some third-rate office. I'd certainly never get one of those plum jobs with an M.P. or an actor."

"What do you want to do?" Joanna asked.

"Ah, that's the whole point—and the reason why you may be such a godsend," Cathy said hopefully. "You see, what I *want* to be is the very last thing they'll let me be. I want to be an actress!"

Joanna regarded her thoughtfully for a moment. "Why?" she asked quietly.

"Oh, I know what you're thinking," Cathy said, with a sigh. "That I'm just another stage-struck teenager. But it isn't that, Joanna, honestly it isn't! I know it's terribly hard work and the chances of success are about two in a million. But I want to try. I want it more than anything."

"Why do you think your mother wouldn't approve?" Joanna asked.

"Because her idea of success is getting married to some-one madly eligible," Cathy said scornfully. "All she wants is for us to catch husbands, preferably important ones. Not that *that* matters much, because it isn't Ma who has to be persuaded."

"Who, then? Your grandmother?"

"Heavens, no! Gran's a lamb. She'd let me start acting tomorrow, if she knew I wanted to. No, it's Charles who's the important one!"

"Charles! But he's not responsible for you," Joanna objected.

"No, not officially. But he's the head of the family now —the one they all kow-tow to."

"But Charles is very fond of you. He might not object, if you explained to him."

"Yes, he would. He'd laugh at me. He thinks I'm still a child," Cathy said earnestly. "But if someone like you could convince him that I'm serious, then he might approve."

"But why me?" Joanna protested. "I've only just arrived. I'm sure Vanessa would be far more likely to influence him."

"Huh, Vanessa!" Cathy gave a hollow laugh. "Haven't you noticed it yet? She and Ma are much too busy with their own scheme."

"What scheme? I don't know what you mean, Cathy," Joanna said perplexedly.

"You will, if you keep your eyes open," Cathy said with a tinge of bitterness. "Vanessa wants to be Mrs. Charles Carlyon. That's why she and Mummy don't like you. They're terrified Charles might fall for you. Oh, it makes me *sick!*"

CHAPTER FOUR

"OH, Cathy, that's absurd! You must be imagining it," Joanna said, as lightly as she could manage.

Cathy scowled at her stockinged feet. "No, I'm not!" she said positively. "Vanessa's absolutely determined to marry him. She practically admitted it to me."

Joanna slipped out of bed and put on her blouse and skirt. "Perhaps she's in love with him," she answered casually. "I should say they were very well matched."

"That's the whole point. She doesn't love him a bit," Cathy said acidly. "She just wants to be rich. I bet she's livid that you've turned out to be so super."

"Thank you," Joanna said drily. "But even if you're right—which I doubt—she hasn't much to worry about. Charles rather dislikes me, as it happens."

"Yes, that's the queerest part," Cathy said thoughtfully. "I saw him watching you at dinner last night, almost as if he were . . . angry with you. Neal thinks you're wonderful, but of course he flirts with almost everyone he meets."

Joanna picked up her hairbrush and began to use it with slow absent-minded strokes. She was troubled, not so much by the subject under discussion, but by Cathy's disillusioned tone. Probably she was imagining the whole affair, or else dramatising it out of all proportion. But even so, her attitude showed that her relationship with her mother and sister was not as it should be.

"Look, to get back to your wanting to go on the sage— there's not much I can do until I've been here a bit longer," she said, after a moment. "You aren't proposing to tell them just yet, are you?"

"No, I suppose not. I've been waiting for the right moment—if it ever comes," the younger girl said gloomily. "But, if I do tell them, you will back me up, won't you?"

Before Joanna could reply, there was a tap at the door

and Vanessa appeared. She was still in her tennis clothes and had a flushed elated look which suited her.

"Oh, hello, Cathy," she said. "I just came up to say that tea is ready," she added to Joanna.

"Thanks. We'll come down," Joanna said with a smile. "Did you have a good game?"

"Yes, marvellous, but Charles is out of practice. I beat him," Vanessa said with a laugh. "What a pity you don't play. You could have joined us."

"Yes, it is," Joanna said mildly.

But if I could play and I wanted to please him, I certainly wouldn't win, she thought to herself.

Aloud, she said, "Oh, Cathy, I'll give you that petticoat. We shan't be long, Vanessa."

"There's no hurry. I'm going to change," her cousin said, disappearing down the corridor.

Joanna went to the chest of drawers and found the petticoat, waving away Cathy's voluble thanks.

"That's all right, you can keep it. I've got another one."

"And you will help me with the other thing?" Cathy asked, glancing over her shoulder at the open door.

"Yes ; if the right moment comes—and if I can," Joanna agreed cautiously.

"You're an angel! I knew you would," Cathy said gratefully. "Come on, let's go and have tea. I'm starving."

Charles was standing by the windows as they entered the drawing-room. He was holding a glass of iced lager and whistling softly. Against the whiteness of his tennis shirt, his arms were brown and muscular. Joanna wondered how he managed to look so fit when most of his life must be spent behind a desk.

"Hello, Charles. Did Van really beat you, or did you let her?" Cathy enquired, helping herself to a sandwich from the trolley.

Charles looked amused. "She trounced me off the court, I'm afraid. She's getting much too good for me," he said.

Cathy looked unconvinced. "I bet you let her. She's not as good as all that," she said, munching.

"Shall I pour you some tea, Cathy?" Joanna asked, hoping to lead the conversation away from this topic.

"No, thanks. I'm going to get some cold squash from the fridge. Shall I get some for you?"

"I'll have tea. It's a taste I should acquire," Joanna said, moving towards the trolley.

For some moments after Cathy's departure, there was silence. Joanna added sugar to her cup and chose a scone. She was not used to being self-conscious and it irked her. What was it about this man that sapped her composure? she wondered resentfully.

"You seem to have made a hit with our infant," he said suddenly, startling her.

She took a second to steady herself, then glance at him. "She's still at the age to take people at their face value," she said coolly. "You probably won't believe it, but I like her."

"Why not? I should say you're not unalike."

Joanna's eyebrows lifted. "What is that supposed to mean?" she asked guardedly.

He set his beer on a table and lit a cigarette. "Nothing uncomplimentary. I'm very fond of her."

"Don't tell me you're revising your opinion of me," Joanna said coolly.

He watched her for a moment without replying, his eyes narrowed and speculative.

"I was forgetting, I have a cheque for you in my other trousers," he said.

Joanna stiffened, her chin lifting. "That won't be necessary," she said crisply. "I've changed my mind."

A faint smile curved his firm mouth. "Mm, I thought you might," he said quietly.

"What do you mean?"

"I rarely make snap decisions—particularly about people," he said. "Whatever else you may be, I don't think you're a profiteer."

She flushed. "Then why did you make your offer?"

He shrugged. "It seemed the quickest means to get you

over here. There's nothing like affronting someone's principles to get a definite reaction. I calculated that you'd either tell me to go to the devil or get some peculiar feminine kick out of playing the part I've offered you."

"You're quite a psychologist, aren't you?" she said stonily. "What if I'd chosen to tell you to go to the devil?"

"Then I should have had to change my tactics," he said carelessly. "But as you were obviously bristling with the most stiff-necked kind of pride it didn't seem very likely."

At this point Cathy returned. But later Joanna remembered what Charles had said and wondered if it were true. She had never thought of herself as a proud person ; unless pride was the resentment she often felt against people whose lives had been easy and who took their circumstances for granted. But surely, when one had had to struggle for everything, it was only natural to be a little scornful of those who had never had to battle for their security? Perhaps not. Perhaps that kind of pride was as much to be disliked as the subtle patronage which she sensed in Vannessa's and her aunt's attitude towards her.

That night, after Charles had left and while they were having coffee in the drawing-room after dinner, Neil suddenly stood up and said, "I think I'll take a run out for an hour or so. How about you, Joanna? Would you like a spot of fresh air after being indoors all day?"

Joanna hesitated, but Mrs. Carlyon said quickly, "Yes, do go, my dear. It will do you good. But don't frighten her out of her wits, Neal. I know how you like to drive, and we don't want an accident when Joanna has only just got here."

"I'll drive as sedately as the vicar, Grandmother," her grandson assured her, grinning. "I should tie a scarf over your hair, Joanna. I'm afraid my old jalopy isn't quite as luxurious as Charles's plushy turn-out."

So Joanna ran upstairs to fetch a jacket and a scarf, and found him waiting for her by the door when she came down. His car was an ancient two-seater, rather cramped for leg room and decidedly draughty, but Joanna did not mind. It was not a chilly evening and she was glad to be out of the house for a while.

"We'll go up on The Ridges," Neal said, as they crunched

77

down the drive. "There's quite a good view of the town from the highest point. Not that the lights of Merefield are likely to uplift you, but at least one escapes the smell of fish and chips and the sound of 'Nellie Dean' being bawled out in the pubs."

"Nellie Dean?" Joanna queried.

He laughed. "It's a song of sorts—not one you'd be likely to want to add to your repertoire, I fancy."

"Oh—so you know."

"Yes, Cathy collared me as soon as I got in and told me. Not that it was much of a surprise. You don't look like a schoolmarm or an office type."

"What do I look like?" she asked, smiling.

She felt him turn his head towards her. "Like the most beautiful girl in Merefield," he said seriously.

She laughed. "Oh, Neal! What a shameless exaggeration. I'm sure Merefield is full of pretty girls—and you've probably said that to all of them. I suspect that you're a terrible flirt."

"Why not? One must get some kick out of life," he said flippantly.

"Is that the only kick you get—playing at love?" she asked.

"Pretty well."

"What about your job?"

"It's a job."

"Charles told me you wanted to be a painter," she said, after a moment.

He swung the car off the main road and up a steep lane. "I considered it," he said in a blank tone.

"What made you give up the idea?"

"I don't subscribe to the theory that genius thrives in a garret," he replied. "Not that I regard myself as a genius, but I might have done something worth while."

"You talk as if it were all over and done with," she said curiously.

"It is."

"But why?" she protested. "If you really want to paint, you can't give it up. It's like music, or dancing, or wanting to go to sea. It's something in your blood. You can't just forget about it."

"Sometimes you have to," he said tersely. "You can't be a sailor if you have to live in a city, and you can't write music if you haven't got a piano."

"But one can paint anywhere," Joanna countered. "You could be painting now."

The road levelled and passed through a tunnel of trees.

"Look," he said quietly, "have you ever heard of a first-class pianist who could only practise for an hour a day, or a ballet dancer who got to the top without training? People seem to think that painting—good painting—is something you either can do or you can't. It's not. It takes years of solid grind to make an artist of any stature. A good picture isn't a lucky chance, it's the result of years of study and practice. Time is what an artist has to have. Time—and something to live on. If I can't do the thing properly, I'd rather not do it at all."

They had come to the end of the trees and, slowing down, Neal turned the car off the road and on to a stretch of rough turf. The beam of the headlamps showed a group of wind-swept pines and, beneath them, a bench. Then he switched off the engine and swung himself out.

The moon was behind a cloud and it was a second or two before Joanna's eyes adjusted to the starlight. Then she saw that they were at the summit of a long bluff, and behind them was a stretch of heathland. Neal held out his hand to her. "You'd better grab a hold. There are quite a few potholes," he said.

His hand was warm and firm and, holding it, she let him lead her across the uneven ground until, as they neared the edge of the cliff, she saw the town. It was spread out beneath them, quite near and yet somehow remote, like a city seen from the air.

"That long curve of blue lights is the by-pass and the red neon sign is the brewery," Neal explained. "Even the railway yards look quite attractive after dark. A pity it isn't dark all the time."

The hardness in his voice chilled her and she shivered.

"Are you cold?" he asked quickly.

"No. It's quite mild," she said. "Where would you live if you could choose, Neal?"

"London," he said at once. "There's something in the air that makes me feel alive. Merefield stifles me. How about you? Where would you live?"

She was silent for a moment, her thoughts winging back to all the places she had been to with her father. Rio . . . Athens . . . Rangoon . . . so many cities, so many memories.

"I don't know," she said softly. "I've never been anywhere that felt like home to me."

The moon emerged from the clouds and he turned to look at her, his fingers tightening. The next moment she was in his arms and he was bending his head to kiss her.

Joanna did not struggle, but she turned her head so that his lips only brushed her cheek.

"What's the matter?" he said. "Don't you like me?"

"I don't know you yet, Neal," she said quietly.

His hold slackened, but he did not release her.

"Don't you like being kissed?" He sounded so puzzled that she almost laughed.

"Not by comparative strangers, I'm afraid," she said mildly. "Is that why you asked me to come out?"

His arms dropped and he let her go. "I'm sorry. I'll take you home." His tone was stiff and offended.

They walked back to the car in silence, and then Joanna touched his sleeve and said, "Don't be so cross about it. I'm not."

He helped her into the car and then walked round the bonnet and slid behind the wheel. But he did not immediately switch on the engine.

"You're a strange girl," he said abruptly, fiddling with the key.

"Why? Because I can resist your fatal fascination?" she asked teasingly. "Or did you assume that, coming from 'gay Paree' and being a night-club entertainer, I would be used to that sort of thing?"

"No, not really. You don't look like a good-time girl," he said, rather gruffly. "I just—oh hell! Now I suppose you'll write me off as a prize heel."

"I don't see why I should," she said mildly. "What little I do know about you, I rather like."

He looked at her. "Really?"

"Yes, really. Anyway, you seem to like me, and that's comforting. I'm not too sure of the others yet," she said wryly.

He seemed about to reply and then changed his mind and started the car.

"Look, how about having a drink somewhere?" he suggested presently.

"All right. But should you, when you're driving?" Joanna asked cautiously.

"One glass of beer won't hurt, and there's quite a decent pub not far from the house," he said, in a more cheerful tone. "Don't worry. I'm no saint, but I haven't started hitting the bottle yet."

The 'pub' proved to be a delightful old coaching inn which had so far been spared the horrors of modernisation. The oak-panelled lounge was empty, but a babel of voices and the sounds of a darts match drifted through the hatch connecting it with the smoke-room. While Joanna sat down on a high-backed settle near the open hearth, Neal ordered a Carlsberg for himself and a Pimm's for her.

"I like this. It's how one imagines England," she said, as he joined her, her glance straying from the sporting prints on the walls to the burnished copper pans above the bar.

"Mm, it's not bad, I suppose. I'd change it for one of your Paris *bistros,* though," he said, with a smile. "Tell me about your work. Presumably this night club is a pretty select one. I can't imagine you prancing around behind a fan."

Joanna looked momentarily puzzled. Then she laughed and said, "Oh, I don't have to do anything like that, thank goodness. All the same, I think some of the people here might not approve of me. My father used to say that the

81

English were the world's greatest hypocrites. When they're abroad they are delighted by anything the least bit shocking, but at home they're very prim. Is that true, do you think?"

Neal grinned. "Probably. I've no doubt old Charles lets down his hair a bit when he's out of the country."

"Charles? Oh, he doesn't strike me as being prim," Joanna said thoughtfully. "He seems a little severe at times, and accustomed to getting what he wants, but I wouldn't have thought him narrow-minded."

"No, close-fistedness is his trouble," Neal said, rather grimly. "He's generous enough with his own money, but he makes darned sure we don't squander any of ours."

"Yours? But what has he to do with your money?" she asked.

"Pretty well everything," Neal replied, with a wry glance. "You see, Grandfather divided his estate among us. Grandmother has the house and the major portion, and my mother has enough to keep her in comfort for the rest of her life. Charles didn't get anything—he doesn't need it. But we three all had equal legacies which we can only use with the trustees' approval. One of the trustees is Mother, but, unfortunately, the other is Charles."

"But the trust can't last for ever. You will be free to spend it as you like eventually, won't you?"

"Oh, yes—eventually," Neal said, with a hollow laugh. "The trust on my money expires when I'm thirty, which is not for five years yet. The girls have to wait till they marry —providing Charles approves their choice of husbands. Of course it was typical of the old man to tie the money up in some way. We expected that. The snag is having Charles as our watch-dog. It's no use getting Mother's consent to a scheme, because he always vetoes it. She can't touch her capital either, she just gets the interest, and of course Grandmother dotes on Charles, so that's out too. In other words, we've got the cash, but we can't use it."

"I see. Yes, that must be very irritating," Joanna agreed thoughtfully. "If you had the money, I suppose you'd go to London and paint?"

"Like a shot from a gun," Neal said gloomily.

"But why does Charles object? Doesn't he think you have enough talent?" she asked.

"Lord knows. He hasn't said so, but I daresay that's the root of it," Neal answered, with a shrug. "His chief objection is that you can't make a living at painting—not until you reach the top flight. I don't give a damn whether I make a living or not, providing I can keep up the rent on a studio and eat occasionally."

Joanna smiled. "But then you've never been poor, have you?" she said gently. "And you haven't only yourself to consider. When you have a wife and children, you can't expect them to live on air."

"Marriage isn't in my scheme of things," Neal said bluntly.

"How can you tell? You aren't immune to falling in love, are you? she asked, with a twinkle.

He laughed. "I daresay not, but that doesn't necessarily involve marriage, does it?"

Joanna's mouth curved. "Not for such a hardened roué, I suppose," she conceded with an impish glance. "I think we should go back now. Grandmother may be anxious about us."

As they went out to the car park, Neal caught her hand and gave it a gentle squeeze. "You're a good sport, Joanna," he said warmly. "By the way, when are you going to be presented to the neighbourhood? You can't spend all your time chatting to Gran."

Joanna had wondered about this herself. Now, on impulse, she said, "To be frank, Neal, I don't think your mother is very anxious to 'present' me, as you put it. Perhaps she's afraid that it may cause a lot of talk. It is rather odd for a stray granddaughter to pop up from nowhere, you know."

"Mm, I suppose it is," he said carelessly. "Of course, poor old Mother's trouble is that she was as jealous as hell of Aunt Nina. I imagine that's why she's a bit chary of you."

"Jealous of my mother? But why?" Joanna asked quickly.

"Well, from all accounts, your mother was a stunner as a girl, and definitely the old boy's favourite before the rumpus," he explained. "Most girls feel a bit green if someone else catches all the attention, and I expect that applies to sisters too."

"Oh, so *that's* it," Joanna said, half to herself.

"What's more, I don't think she's too happy at having you arrive at a strategic moment," Neal added, opening the door of the car for her.

Joanna waited for him to settle himself beside her.

"What do you mean by that?"

"Haven't you caught on yet?" he asked, with an amused glance. "Mamma is nursing fond hopes that when his lordship finally gets around to marriage, he won't look too far for his bride. Charles and Vanessa," he added, in case she hadn't followed him. "Mind you, if he's got any sense, he'll foil her maternal schemes. I'm not exactly devoted to Charles, but I think he could do better than to pick Van."

"What a strange thing to say. Aren't you fond of her?" Joanna asked.

"Oh, yes, I'm fond of her," Neal said airily. "But that doesn't blind me to her failings. Vanessa's the kind of girl who, if you made a pass at her"—he shot a laughing glance at her—"would either fell you with a nifty left hook or tell you not to mess up her hair."

"Well, I rather doubt if Charles makes passes at girls unless he's reasonably sure of the outcome," Joanna said. "Actually Cathy did mention something about Vanessa being fond of him to me. Will they be getting engaged quite soon, do you suppose?"

"Ah, now that's the prize question," Neal said, putting the car in gear and waiting for a lorry to pass. "So far there's been no sign of Charles capitulating. I think Mother's afraid he may prefer his freedom. He's been quite a gay dog in his day, but it's never got as far as marriage. Possibly it never will. Can't say I blame him. He's got a first-class housekeeper. Why should he take a wife?"

Joanna laughed and accused him of being a cynic, and presently they drew up outside Mere House and went indoors. Mrs. Carlyon and her daughter had gone to bed, but Vanessa was still in the drawing-room, reading a book. She looked up as they entered and her eyes rested thoughtfully on her brother as he helped Joanna to remove her jacket.

"Grandmother is going to give a party for you, Joanna," she said. "She's been discussing it with Mummy all evening. She asked me to tell you about it when you came in."

"That's very kind of her. But won't it make a great deal of work for your mother?" Joanna said uncertainly.

"Oh, Mummy won't mind. She loves organising things," Vanessa said pleasantly. Her manner was suddenly so cordial that Joanna was quite nonplussed.

"What sort of party? Mother's cronies, or a free-for-all?" Neal enquired.

"Quite a mixed list, I think," Vanessa answered. "Gran suggested that I should ask the Forbes twins and Mary Lester, and perhaps you could produce some men. There's going to be a small dinner party first and then a buffet and dancing for the latecomers."

Neal raised his eyebrows. "Quite a shindig, by the sound of it. Gran seems to have taken on a new lease of life since you arrived, Joanna. This house isn't exactly renowned for its merry-making."

"Have you brought a party dress with you, Joanna?" Vanessa asked.

"Yes, I think I have a dress which will do—unless it's going to be a very grand occasion," Joanna said, still greatly perplexed by her cousin's change of front. "What will you wear, Vanessa?"

"I think it's time I had a new evening dress," Vanessa said. "I'll have a look round the shops tomorrow. As Neal says, it's not often that we have a party here, although there are several good dances in the town during the winter."

She began to question Joanna about the price and quality of clothes and accessories in Paris, but although her interest in the subject appeared to be genuine, Joanna had the uncomfortable conviction that it was part of an act, the purpose of which she was at a loss to divine.

Perhaps Neal also sensed this, or perhaps he was bored by a topic which excluded him. At any rate, it was not long before he suggested that they should go to bed.

The following morning, Joanna was invited to accompany her aunt and Vanessa into Merefield for shopping and morning coffee.

It seemed that Mrs. Durrant had also had a change of heart towards her niece ; as Joanna went upstairs to put on street clothes, she felt more than ever confused by this sudden *volte-face*.

Changing her dress for a suit of caramel linen, she pinned on a lighter straw pill-box and found the gloves that matched it. Then, stepping into plain calf pumps, she checked the contents of her bag and added a clean handkerchief.

Her cousin was waiting in the hall when she went downstairs.

"Mummy's seeing Alice about the grocery order. She won't be long," Vanessa said, her eyes on Joanna's suit. "You needn't have bothered to dress up," she added, looking away.

"Oh—do I look wrong for shopping?" Joanna asked anxiously.

Vanessa gave her another swift glance. "It doesn't matter particularly," she said, with a shrug. "We go in for country clothes, but I suppose you haven't got any."

Joanna looked at her cousin's floral shirtwaister and pastel cardigan.

"No, I'm afraid I haven't," she said awkwardly.

Mrs. Durrant came out of the kitchen. She too was wearing a flower-patterned dress under a knitted jacket. She too appraised her niece with a hint of censure, although she made no remark.

Sitting in the back of the car, Joanna tried not to mind their disapproval. But, as they parked the car in a side street and mingled with the other shoppers, she was uncomfortably conscious that people were eyeing her and even turning round to stare. At the grocery shop Mrs. Durrant chose bacon and cheese, and left a list of other provisions to be delivered. Then they went to the library to change Mrs. Carlyon's books for her. By this time it was nearing eleven, and her aunt led the way into a large department store where they took a lift to the top floor restaurant.

It was already crowded with women, and as they made their way to a corner table, Mrs. Durrant nodded and smiled to many of them and stopped once or twice to exchange a greeting. But, although it was apparent that they were curious about her, Joanna noticed that her aunt did not wait for an introduction to become necessary.

"Oh, there are Angela and her mother. I want to ask her something. I shan't be a minute," Vanessa said, as they were about to sit down. And, leaving them, she hurried over to a distant table where a middle-aged woman and a young girl were sitting.

Mrs. Durrant drew off her gloves and ordered three coffees, her eyes ranging over the room to see who else was present. She had not spoken to Joanna since they left the house, and her niece began to think that her unexpected friendliness at breakfast time had been assumed for Mrs. Carlyon's benefit.

Suddenly her aunt gave an exclamation of surprise and said, "Why, here's Charles. I wonder what he wants?"

Joanna looked up and saw Charles coming towards them between the tables.

"Good morning," he said pleasantly. "I thought I'd find you here. Can I join you?"

"Why, of course. We're delighted to see you," Mrs. Durrant said, looking pleased. "Vanessa has just gone over to speak to Angela Maybury. She won't be long. Did Mother tell you where we were?"

Charles sat down opposite Joanna and cast a faintly derisive eye round the groups of chattering women.

"Yes, she phoned me about this party you're throwing, and as I had half an hour to spare I thought I'd come up and find you." He glanced at Joanna. "You're looking very chic this morning. I'm afraid it won't endear you to the local matrons."

Joanna coloured slightly and kept silent.

"It's a pity Mother didn't mention the idea when you were with us, Charles," her aunt said briskly. "I tried to dissuade her from it, but she got quite worked up, so I was obliged to agree. It's not that I mind arranging it, but I'm wondering if it's likely to be too much for her. It isn't as if Joanna were going to be with us for long. I'm sure she doesn't mind whether she meets our friends or not."

"No, I daresay she doesn't, but Grandmother seems very set on it, so we may as well please her," Charles said easily. "What would you like me to do? Lay on the drinks?"

"Yes, if you would. And we'd better go over the guest list together. It's very short notice for everyone, I'm afraid," Mrs. Durrant said with a frown. "Ah, here's Vanessa."

Charles rose to his feet and drew out a chair for Vanessa, who greeted him with evident pleasure.

"I thought you disapproved of our morning coffee sessions, Charles?" she remarked.

Her cousin shrugged his broad shoulders, his glance ranging over the groups of chattering women with a glint of sardonic amusement.

"I wouldn't put it as strongly as that," he said negligently. Then, turning to Joanna, "You probably haven't realised it, but this is one of the sacred rituals of the English middle classes—an hour's gossip over what passes for coffee every morning."

"I don't know why you should be so scathing about it, Charles. It seems to be a very harmless practice, and I've no doubt Frenchwomen also meet for coffee at mid-morning," said Mrs. Durrant.

"Do they, Joanna?" he enquired.

"I really don't know," she replied uncertainly. "I was usually still in bed at this time, and I didn't mix with many married women."

"Who did you know?" Vanessa asked curiously.

"Oh, the other girls in the cabaret and the customers at the café where I lived. They were mostly local tradesmen and stall-holders from the flower market," Joanna explained unthinkingly.

"Indeed," Mrs. Durrant said frigidly.

If one had been obliged to live over an artisans' café and mingle with the customers, one could at least have the sensibility not to dwell on such circumstances—that was clearly her aunt's view of the subject.

Such empty snobbishness set Joanna's teeth on edge. The patrons of the Bernadine might not be as consciously refined as Merefield's coffee groups, but at least they were honest and kindly and amusing, she thought angrily. Another pang of longing for French faces and voices took hold of her. She wished she had never come to Merefield, never let Charles goad her into shelving her plans for Brittany.

As soon as they had all drunk their coffee, Mrs. Durrant asked Charles to signal to their waitress.

"We must be getting on if you want to look at dresses, Vanessa. Perhaps you'll look in this evening so that we can discuss the details of this party, Charles."

He accompanied them to the street where he said good-bye and strode away to the car park. A few minutes earlier, in the lift, Joanna had found his eyes resting on her with an expression she could not fathom. She wondered if he too had thought her remarks in bad taste.

Neither of the Durrants consulted her opinion in the choice of Vanessa's dress, although the saleswomen at the various shops they visited made several abortive attempts to draw her into the discussion. Finally, when it was drawing close to lunch-time, her cousin made up her mind to have a simple low-necked dress in shaded pink-and-white poult. Joanna thought privately that it was a rather insipid design and, had she been her cousin, she would have settled for a cheaper but more dashing style in subtle chartreuse cotton. But Mrs. Durrant evidently saw her daughter as the "English rose" type and had dismissed the more sophisticated style as being too old for her.

While the fitter made adjustments to the shoulders, Joanna wondered if this emphatic outdoor-girl rosiness was really most likely to appeal to Charles's taste. She now had little doubt that Cathy was right in her view of her mother's matrimonial ambitions.

*   *   *

It was arranged that the party should take place on the following Saturday. Charles seemed to have decided that she no longer needed his supervision, and Joanna saw little of him during the remainder of the week. But she did go for two more evening runs with Neal, and her liking for him increased. In a way, he reminded her of Yves, although

89

he lacked the Frenchman's polish and suavity. Neal's worldliness was only a veneer, she guessed.

On the night of the party, she had taken a bath and was fastening her dressing-gown when there was a rap on the door and Neal called, "Get a move on, Van! You've been in there hours. What about the rest of us?"

Joanna gathered up her things and unlocked the door. "It's me. Have I held you up? I'm sorry, Neal," she said with a smile.

His glance swept from the white chiffon bandeau on her hair to her green velvet mules. His scowl of impatience gave place to an appreciative grin.

"Me . . . you smell delicious," he said, inhaling. "Actually you must have been very quick. The last time I rattled the door, Vanessa was still wallowing."

Joanna laughed. "That's one of the penalties of living with a houseful of women—you can never get to the bathroom."

She moved to pass him, but he put out a hand and held her arm. "Don't dash away for a minute. I'd always been led to believe that girls looked terrible without their war-paint. That certainly doesn't apply to you. Your skin's like silk."

"Thank you. All the same I don't think I'll appear downstairs without some camouflage," she said, amused.

"You certainly don't need it." He drew in another deep breath. "What's the scent? An expensive present from some rich admirer at the cabaret?"

"It's Balmain's 'Jolie Madame'—and I bought it myself," she said drily.

"Well, I don't know what you're planning to wear, but any girl with that stuff behind her ears could put on a sack and still have the men dropping like ninepins. The local belles don't run to anything more intoxicating than lavender water," he said, with a wry expression.

"French scent is very expensive in England," she pointed out.

"Probably—but they could always save on something else." His eyes glinted with mischief. "You'll be a knock-out with the male element, my dear Joanna, but the women are going to hate you."

"I hope not. I don't see why they should," Joanna said anxiously. Then a faint glimmer of amusement lit her eyes. "You're not expecting me to come down in one of my cabaret costumes, are you?"

"I only wish you would—that would really get their claws out," he said wickedly. "But you won't need a scanty dress to set their teeth on edge. That subtle Parisian gloss will be enough." His hand tightened and he moved a little closer. "Though at the moment, in that kimono thing, you look more like some ravishing little geisha girl."

"Oh, Neal, you're incorrigible!" Joanna broke into laughter.

"What's so funny?" he asked, looking slightly injured at this hilarious reception of his compliment.

"You are! If you had a moustache, I believe you'd be twirling it at me." She put up her free hand and, twisting imaginary whiskers, said in a throaty voice, " 'Aha, me pretty village maid, and where are you off to?' "

Neal was not amused. "I'm sorry," he said gruffly, "I can't compete with your usual smooth Latin boy-friends, I'm afraid."

Joanna found this retort even funnier, but, seeing that he was really offended, she stifled another burst of laughter and said gently, "Oh, don't be huffy, Neal. I haven't any smooth Latin boy-friends—they sound odious!—and I much prefer nice un-smooth Englishmen."

And then, because he was still looking rather wounded, and because it was endearing to see that he was so much less confident than he pretended, she reached up and brushed a light, friendly kiss against his cheek. At that precise moment Mrs. Durrant reached the top of the stairs and turned towards them.

Neal saw his mother first and there was a rather peculiar expression on his face as he met her cold regard. After fixing a repressive glance on her son for some seconds, Mrs. Durrant looked freezingly at her niece. And, much to her chagrin, Joanna felt her cheeks beginning to burn. Nobody spoke, but the tension was almost tangible.

The painful silence might have stretched out indefinitely had not Cathy come out of her room to find someone to unstick a zipper. As she saw her mother's expression, her voice tailed off and she shot a curious look at the other two, her tussle with the fastener forgotten as she sensed the chill of the atmosphere.

"I'll come and deal with it in a moment, Cathy," Mrs. Durrant said, her tone very clipped and precise. Then, to her son: "If you're intending to shave again, Neal, please be as quick as you can. I shall want the bathroom myself in a few minutes."

"Right, I'll get a move on." Neal flickered a half smile at Joanna and disappeared into the bathroom. Whether he had been amused, embarrassed or exasperated by his mother's reading of the situation was impossible to tell.

For an instant it seemed as if Mrs. Durrant was about to say something else. But, with tightened lips and veiled eyes, she ignored Joanna and hustled Cathy back into her bedroom. Almost, Joanna thought with a mingling of annoyance and amusement, as if she were shielding her innocent offspring from contact with a Scarlet Woman.

Back in her own room, she leaned against the door for a moment. She was still vexed with herself for having coloured like a guilty schoolgirl. A fine start to the evening, she thought bleakly, as she put away her toilet things. But as she sat down at the dressing-table to do her face, her sense of humour overcame her irritation. Her aunt could not have behaved more censoriously if she had surprised them together in the most abandoned embrace. She must either be inordinately prudish or else her detestation of me overcomes all common sense, Joanna reflected, with a wry quirk of her mouth.

A light tap at the door distracted her as she was applying foundation cream. Was it her aunt, come to deliver a frigid homily on the impropriety of her behaviour? Or Neal? Or an inquisitive Cathy?

Instead of calling her visitor to come in, Joanna crossed the room.

"Who is it?" she asked through the door.

"It's Neal." His voice was low and urgent. "Can I see you?"

The idiot! If his mother caught him lurking stealthily outside this door, she would be even more furious.

"I'm in the middle of dressing. I'll see you downstairs," Joanna answered in a casual tone.

There was no further sound and, after waiting for some moments, she concluded that he had accepted her refusal and gone away.

It took her nearly half an hour to put on her make-up and brush her hair into a smooth French pleat at the back of her head. Then, shedding the kimono, she went to the wardrobe and took out the dress she had finally chosen to wear. At first she had been tempted to wear something that would confirm her aunt's suspicions and fan any highly-coloured rumours that might be circulating about her life in Paris. There would have been a wicked satisfaction in playing out the part they had doubtless assigned to her—that of the ne'er-do-well Michael Allen's shameless daughter whom Charles had found in some scandalous Pigalle "dive." And provoking Charles would have been particularly satisfactory. She knew just the way his dark eyebrows would lift, his lips compress. It was her regard for her grandmother which had made her choose the least dashing of her dresses. Indeed, as she slipped the garment from its hanger and opened the long slide fastener beneath the sleeve, she wondered if this dress might not be too plain, its elegance too understated to appeal to local taste. The dress was made of an unusual shade of grey-green otto-man, the colour and sheen like that of a pigeon's wing. The design was very simple: a high neckline, long tight sleeves and a slender skirt. The fact that, at the back, it was cut away to the base of her shoulder-blades could scarcely offend anyone.

She had stepped into the matching glacé slippers and was screwing on amethyst ear-rings, when Cathy tapped at the door and popped her head round.

"Can I come in? Are you ready?"

Joanna smiled at her. "I will be in a moment. You look very nice."

"Honestly? You don't think this dress is too babyish?" Cathy postured critically in front of the long mirror on the wardrobe door. She was wearing lemon voile in a charming

Victorian style. "How about me?" she asked. "Will I pass muster, do you think?"

Cathy eyed the grey silk. "You always look nice," she said politely. Then, after a second of hesitation, "I was hoping you were going to put on something really sizzling."

Joanna grinned. "Skin-tight lamé with practically no top, I suppose?"

Cathy giggled. "Well, not quite as sizzling as *that*," she admitted. "But something more . . . more *French*."

Joanna's lips twitched as she tucked a compact and handkerchief into a small mesh bag. "I'll sizzle for you some other night," she said gaily. "This evening I just want to merge with the background."

"How does your hair stay up like that?" Cathy began, turning and running to the window as the sound of a car turning in at the gate was heard.

"It's Charles," she announced over her shoulder, as the engine was switched off.

Neal was leaning against the balustrade at the head of the stairs as they left the room. The severe black and white of his evening kit emphasised his fair good looks. As Cathy ran down the stairs, calling to Charles, Neal stopped Joanna from following her by catching her wrist.

"You look very demure. I was expecting a Paris model," he said with a hint of disappointment in his voice.

"So was Cathy. You aren't exactly boosting my morale," she replied drily.

"I didn't mean that you don't look nice," he said hastily. 'You always do. But I'd been looking forward to seeing you stun 'em. By the way, I'm sorry if Mother embarrassed you earlier on. I think she was mainly annoyed at finding me hanging about when she wanted to use the bathroom."

"Yes, I expect so. She's had a hectic day," Joanna said noncommittally. "Shall we go down?"

Charles was still in the hall as they turned the bend of the stairs. He looked up at them and Joanna saw his eyes sweep over her. Would he too express surprise at her choice of dress?

When he made no comment at all, she found herself

94

slightly piqued. Somehow she had expected that Charles would approve her discretion and like the dress for itself. Evidently she had been mistaken.

However, she was a good deal heartened when her grandmother, who was already seated in the drawing-room, said warmly, "You look most delightful, my dear. I shall be very proud of you."

Joanna was still talking to Mrs. Carlyon when the two other women came down and a few minutes later the first guests arrived, so she was not a witness of Charles's greeting to Vanessa. The pleased smile which animated her cousin's face as she stood beside her mother in the hall to welcome their visitors suggested that his reaction to her appearance had been a gratifying one.

For the following hour, Joanna was kept busy making small-talk to the people to whom she was introduced. This was something of an ordeal, as very few of them could wholly conceal that their curiosity about her went deeper than the normal interest of a newcomer to their set. One or two of Mrs. Carlyon's contemporaries spoke kindly of Joanna's mother and remarked upon the likeness between them. This she did not mind. But the delicately probing questions and the avid appraisals of some of her aunt's cronies made her temper simmer.

She was relieved when Neal came to take her to dance.

"I believe they're half expecting me to break into a can-can or a strip-tease," she said a shade crossly, as they began to quickstep. "It's obviously no secret that I worked in a night club."

"Nothing's ever secret in a town this size," he said wryly. "Why let it bother you? They're probably as envious as hell."

Joanna smiled and relaxed. It was silly to be irritated, she decided. Probably if she had spent most of her life in a quiet provincial town, she too would be wildly intrigued by the sudden revival of an old local scandal.

Over Neal's shoulder she saw Charles dancing with an elderly woman in black lace. His well-shaped dark head was slightly inclined as he listened to his partner's remarks. Suddenly, as if he sensed that someone was watching him, he glanced up. Joanna smiled at him, but although he acknowledged the smile with a faint upward tilt of his lips, there was no answering warmth in the keen grey eyes. Feeling oddly hurt by his unfriendliness, Joanna hastily switched her attention back to Neal, and for the remainder of the dance she was careful not to look in that direction again.

Presently people began to drift towards the supper-room, and she found herself talking to a pleasant young married couple, the Drurys, who wanted to know if she could recommend a cheap *pension* where they could spend their next holiday.

"I love your dress, Miss Allen," said Margaret Drury, after her husband had gone to fetch them some fruit sorbets. "I used to work in London before I was married, you know, and in the first six months up here I nearly went mad with frustration. There's pots of money in this town, but the standard of taste is abysmal. The shops never seem to catch up with fashions until they're completely outmoded, and if you ask for any new line they tell you there's no demand for it."

"There's nothing outdated about that dress you're wearing," Joanna said, smiling. Margaret's coral chiffon had caught her eye some time earlier.

"Well, fortunately I'm fairly handy with a sewing-machine, so I try not to get too dowdy," the other girl explained. "Not that I go out much nowadays, because it's so horribly expensive to hire a baby-sitter."

"Oh, you have children?" Joanna asked politely.

"Only one—but he's more than enough to cope with for the moment," Margaret said.

"How old is he?"

"Ten months—but already a holy terror," said a voice from behind her.

Turning, Joanna found Charles smiling at Margaret over her head.

"Charles is the brat's godfather, so he's entitled to malign him," Margaret said, laughing. "You haven't been to see us for ages, Charles. Are your godson's bellows beginning to wear your nerves?"

"I've been tied up lately. I'll look in tomorrow if I may."

96

"Come to supper. You know you're always welcome," Margaret said warmly. She turned to Joanna. "Perhaps you'd like to come too, Miss Allen, if you're not already booked and you can stand my infant's howls. He's teething, poor lamb."

Joanna flickered an uncertain glance at Charles, but he was crushing out his cigarette, so she had no means of deducing whether he wished her to accept.

"I'd like to," she said, after a fractional pause.

"Good. We'll expect you about seven. Oh, Dick, I've just asked Charles and Miss Allen to share pot luck with us tomorrow."

Her husband put the sorbets on the table beside them and gave Joanna a grin. "You'd better bring some ear-plugs and some form of protective covering, Miss Allen. Maggie doesn't stand on ceremony and you're quite likely to find yourself with a soaking wet infant on your lap. Everyone's seconded to help when things get too hectic."

"Even Charles?" Joanna asked impishly. Somehow she could not imagine him coping with a screaming and soggy infant.

"Oh, Charles is a dab hand with nappies—even better than Dick," Margaret said earnestly. "In fact, if he hadn't been with us when Bunter was about a fortnight old, the poor little wretch would probably have choked to death. Dick and I were wringing our hands in panic and Charles just heaved him upside down and batted him back to normal."

"I dare say I should have panicked too if it had been my own child," Charles said negligently, but with a glint of mockery at Joanna's surprised look.

"You'll never have any if you don't hurry up and find a wife," Margaret said candidly. "It's all very well being a carefree bachelor now, but it won't be so pleasant when you're old and crotchety and need someone to poultice your lumbago."

"You stick to your guns, old chap," Dick advised him. "I'm not saying that marriage hasn't some advantages if the girl can cook decently and has a proper respect for her lord and master. Otherwise you're just putting your head

97

in a noose which gets tighter every year. Look at me, if you've any doubts. Five years ago I hadn't a care in the world. Now I'm up to my neck in hire purchase payments, and I'm lucky if I get a clean shirt once a month. I can't see you living on corned beef sandwiches and darning your own socks."

"Just for that you can have the pleasure of crawling out of bed at half-past five to make up Bunter's early bottle," Margaret retorted crisply, but with a wink at Joanna.

"You see?" Dick said dolefully. "She's henpecking me already. In another few years I'll be completely down-trodden."

Joanna smiled at their banter, but with a curious inner pang. It was very clear that several years of marriage and the stress of coping with their first child had not yet dulled their feelings for each other. They could afford to mock their happiness because, even if there was an element of truth in their raillery, they had something which was proof against every hazard. How safe Margaret must feel, she thought rather wistfully.

"You're looking very serious, Joanna," Charles said suddenly, catching her out in the middle of this thought.

"She's begun to have doubts about the certainty of wedded bliss," suggested Dick.

Joanna laughed, but her cheeks were faintly flushed. "Of course not!" she said quickly. "I—I was envying you a little."

Both Dick and Margaret gave a shout of laughter, but Charles's eyes narrowed and Joanna wished she had not made the admission. He probably thought she was over-playing her rôle and despised her for the insincerity.

"You wait till you've seen how we live. You'll probably wonder we survive at all," Margaret prophesied cheerfully.

At this point they were joined by Vanessa, who exchanged a few words with the Drurys before saying, "Charles, could you spare a moment? Mother would like a word with you."

"Of course. Will you excuse me?" Slipping a hand under Vanessa's elbow, he followed her out of the room.

Both Margaret and Dick watched them leave.

"Vanessa looks very nice tonight," Dick said, after a moment.

"Yes, doesn't she?" A man would have accepted Margaret's agreement, but Joanna knew at once that his wife did not like her cousin.

After supper the party showed a marked division. The older guests congregated in the morning-room to talk, while the younger visitors returned to the drawing-room where Neal had put a jazzier selection of records on the radiogram. Joanna danced with Dick Drury and then with a redhaired boy who probably wanted to jive but wasn't sure of her reaction. His deferential manner made Joanna feel that she ought to be in the morning-room with the parents and grandparents.

About eleven o'clock there was another break for refreshments and someone began to strum on the piano, picking out the latest pop song.

"How about providing an impromptu cabaret, Joanna?" Neal suggested, suddenly appearing beside her. "Andrew's a first-rate pianist. Just name the tune and he'll play it for you."

"Oh no, I couldn't!" Joanna said swiftly, shaking her head.

But several people had overheard the suggestion and her refusal was drowned in a chorus of approval. "Jolly good idea!" "Come on, Miss Allen." "What's the latest hit in Paris?"

Joanna bit her lip, furious with Neal for proposing it, and gripped by an unreasonable alarm at the thought of being forced into the limelight.

"No, really, I don't think . . ." she began uncertainly.

"Now don't pretend you're shy," Neal said, grinning.

And before she could protest more vigorously, he had seized her hand and was leading her towards the piano.

Realising that, short of being markedly ungracious, there was no way out of the situation, Joanna stood, inwardly fuming, while he rapped on the lid of the piano to attract attention.

"Ladies and gentlemen—a surprise! As you may know,

our cousin Joanna is the star of a top French cabaret, and she's going to sing for us tonight."

A murmur of interest and a patter of polite applause followed the announcement. Joanna, her mind suddenly blank, tried desperately to think of a suitable song.

There was now an expectant silence and she was dreadfully conscious that at any moment the people in the morning-room would notice the sudden hush and come to investigate.

"How about 'La Vie en Rose'?" the boy at the piano murmured helpfully, evidently sensing her confusion.

Grateful for any lead, since all she could think of was a French nursery jingle, Joanna nodded and hoped that she could remember the lyric. Someone—presumably Neal—had switched out all but one of the lights, and as she forced herself to relax, she was wretchedly certain that her aunt was going to be furious about this development.

It was a measure of comfort to find that the boy named Andrew was indeed a very good pianist, and as he played an introduction, Joanna got a grip on herself and ignored the battery of eyes upon her. The song was an old one, but it had a pretty lilting melody and she sang it in French, very softly and simply. If they expected the standardised gyrations of a third-rate torch singer, they would be disappointed.

At the end there was a burst of clapping. Joanna bowed, smiled her thanks to Andrew, and stepped quickly away from the piano. But on all sides people were urging her to sing something else, and a moment later, the youngsters nearest the piano began to make room for their hostess and elders to join them. With sinking spirits, Joanna saw Charles shepherding her grandmother towards her.

"Oh, *do* sing again, my dear," Mrs. Carlyon said delightedly. "We only realised what was happening a few moments ago, so we missed most of that pretty French song."

Joanna looked briefly at Charles and saw a faintly ironical gleam in his eyes. He was probably enjoying her discomfiture, she thought furiously. Just behind him, her aunt was forcing a thin smile, but her nostrils were taut with annoyance.

100

Something about that false smile set Joanna's temper simmering. There were time when her father's impetuous blood ran hot and fast in her—and this was one of them! Why should she worry so much about what these people thought of her? With the exception of her grandmother, and perhaps Cathy and Neal, none of them meant a thing to her. So why fall over backwards to make a good impression?

Turning to Andrew, she said, "If I try something new, can you follow me in?"

"I'll try."

"Fine!" She faced her audience. "It's a little difficult without music, but we'll do our best," she said, smiling. "This song is a new one and it hasn't crossed the Channel yet, so I'm afraid I'll have to sing in French again."

The song was really a completely innocuous ballad about spring-time and youthful romance—but no one without a good command of French would have guessed this. Deliberately, Joanna sang it in a manner calculated to give quite another impression. Lounging indolently against the piano, her eyelids drooping, she purred her way through the lyric in what was actually a flagrant parody of the most synthetic type of *chanteuse*. Had Gustave Hugo been present, he would have roared with laughter.

Perhaps, if she had not glanced at Mrs. Durrant again, Joanna might not have carried the burlesque as far as she did. But the sight of her aunt looking so acutely distasteful only spurred her on. Launching into the second verse, she noticed a jolly-looking old man who was sitting not far from the piano, and perched herself on his knee. Fortunately he was as jocular as he looked, and seemed rather pleased to have been singled out. At any rate, he chuckled delightedly while she sang to him, and gave her an enthusiastic squeeze round the waist before she moved away.

Avoiding Neal, who would obviously have been delighted to co-operate, Joanna saw Vanessa and Charles on the other side of the room. Vanessa was looking as appalled as her mother, but Charles seemed rather amused. This was unexpected and, perverse as it might be, Joanna felt disapponted. She knew he had too much control to show open displeasure, but she had certainly hoped to kindle a retaliatory glint. Perhaps he'd show some reaction if she brought him into the act.

There was a bowl of roses on top of the piano. She snapped off a bud and, still vamping outrageously, swayed over Charles. With a provocative smile, she brushed the flower lightly down his cheek, then slipped the stem through his buttonhole.

Someone—probably Neal—gave a shout of laughter, and there was a stifled giggle from one of the girls. But Charles didn't bat an eyelid. What he did do was to catch hold of Joanna's wrist as she was about to withdraw her hand, and although it probably looked the lightest of clasps to the onlookers, his fingers were actually as steely as a manacle.

For an instant, Joanna was tempted to call his bluff and pull away. But as if he read the thought, he increased the pressure of his thumb inside her wrist. Furious, but determined not to show it, she was obliged to finish the song with her hand still captive. And it wasn't easy to look up into his face and croon words of love when she felt like kicking his shins.

At last the song was over, and there was another burst of applause. Whether or not it had been recognised as such, the burlesque had gone down very well.

"Having fun?" Charles murmured, in an undertone, as he released her wrist to join in the clapping.

Joanna stepped back to the piano, bowed, thanked Andrew for his accompaniment, and firmly declined to give an encore.

By midnight, most of the older guests had left and Monica Durrant had escorted her mother to bed. However, Mrs. Carlyon had left instructions that the younger people were to go on dancing as long as they liked, and it was after one before the party began to break up.

"Like a breather?" Neal asked, when his sister had gone into the hall to see off the last couple.

Joanna nodded. Charles was talking to Cathy, who had been allowed to stay up so late as an end-of-term celebration. Joanna hoped that by going outside with Neal she could avoid another encounter with him.

"Enjoy yourself?" her cousin asked, as they strolled across the lawn.

She nodded. But she hadn't enjoyed it at all, and now that it was over, she felt oddly tired and overstrung. The first faint prick of a headache was beginning to tighten her temples.

Neal tucked her hand through his arm. "You certainly made a hit with the Brigadier. The poor old boy probably hasn't had his arm round a pretty girl since the Great War," he said, chuckling. "I wished you'd picked on me instead of Charles," he added, squeezing her arm against his side.

"It was entirely your fault that I had to sing in the first place," Joanna said, yawning.

"You didn't really mind, did you? You can't possibly be shy if you do it for a living."

"I'm supposed to be on holiday at the moment."

"Well, I wouldn't have landed you in for it if I'd thought you were genuinely reluctant," he said anxiously. "But it did give the party no end of a lift, you know. People will be talking about it for weeks."

"That I don't doubt," Joanna said drily.

"Oh, look here, you aren't in a fret because Ma didn't care for it, are you? That's just silly. I admit she looked pretty frosty—and Van was obviously livid when you latched on to Charles—but why worry about them? Gran was tickled pink, and so was everyone else."

"Don't you like your mother, Neal?" Joanna asked curiously.

"Not much," he admitted bluntly.

"But that's dreadful. It's . . . it's unnatural!" she protested.

"I don't see why," he said carelessly. "Just because someone's your parent, it doesn't follow that you're bound to hit it off with them. If married couples can get on each other's nerves—and they choose to live together, remember—why not parents and offspring? Frankly, Ma maddens me. She makes such a fetish of appearances—doing and saying the right thing, conforming to what is or isn't 'done'."

"But you must have *some* affection for her."

"No, I haven't," he said flatly. "Cathy is the only one I've cared about since Dad died. Van's too like Ma."

Joanna was horrified. Even though she had no liking for Mrs. Durrant herself, it seemed terrible for Neal to lack any fondness for her. She had read somewhere that although, in a normal family, affection was fairly equal between all the members, there was always a special bond between sons and mothers and fathers and daughters.

"Tell me about your father," she said gently.

"Dad? Oh, *he* was first-rate," Neal answered swiftly. "I suppose that's why I can't stick Ma," he added, with a shrug. "She pretty well finished him off."

"What on earth do you mean by that?"

"That's what it amounted to," Neal went on coldly. "She didn't swipe him with the coal shovel—nothing so vulgarly emotional. She just nagged him to death, which is a hell of a lot worse, if you ask me. Lord knows why she married him. He wasn't really up to her precious standards. Maybe he was the only chap who asked her. Anyway, once they were hitched, she started moulding him. You know what they say about every successful man having a woman behind him—well, that was Ma's idea. The trouble was that Dad wasn't cut out for her kind of success. He did his best, but it was never quite good enough. So first he got ulcers and, finally, coronary thrombosis." His voice was suddenly husky, and he cleared his throat. "I don't know why I'm boring you with all this," he said, more lightly. "I didn't bring you out here to brood!"

Joanna thought it wise to follow the cue. "Why did you bring me out?" she asked, with a smile. Poor Neal, she thought inwardly. It was obvious that he had adored his father and, if Mrs. Durrant's insistent ambitions had been a contributory factor in her husband's death, it was no wonder that her son felt bitter and disillusioned.

They had passed out of the shelter of the thick yew hedge that bordered one side of the lawn, and a breeze rustled the leaves of the beech tree.

"I say, you must be cold. Slip this on," Neal said concernedly. And before she could object, he had stripped off his dinner jacket and draped it round her shoulders.

104

"What about you?" she protested. "That dress shirt is no warmer than my frock."

"Ah, but I'm a rugged male," he answered, grinning.

There was the sound of a car starting up at the front of the house.

"That must be Charles going off. I wonder if Van has managed to bring him up to scratch?" Neal speculated. "I have an idea that she and Ma were expecting tonight to be the night."

Joanna didn't comment. "We'd better go in and get some sleep," she suggested, turning back towards the house.

The lights in the drawing-room had been switched off and this side of the house was in darkness. But there was enough moonlight for them to see their way.

"Hope Van hasn't locked the fresh doors or we shall have to scale the ivy," Neal remarked. But as they neared the terrace they could see that the doors were still wide open.

At the foot of the terrace steps, Neal caught her hand and made her stop short.

"What is it?" she whispered, lowering her tone because Mrs. Carlyon's bedroom was above the drawing-room and normal voices might carry on the quiet night air and disturb her.

Neal moved closer and slid an arm round her waist. "Look, just because we're not a very united family, I don't want you to think I'm completely cold-blooded," he murmured. "The best parties usually wind up with a little dalliance, you know."

Joanna stifled a laugh. "Oh, Neal, you're hopeless! Why didn't you dally with that pretty little blonde in white? She looked as if she'd welcome it."

"Because I'd rather dally with you." His arm tightened, his other hand tipping up her chin.

Afterwards, Joanna wasn't sure whether she would have let him kiss her or not. It would have been comforting to have been held close for a moment or two, and she knew Neal wasn't serious. Like herself, he wanted a little affection.

As it happened, the decision was taken out of her hands

105

by the sudden flare of a lighter from a shadowed corner of the terrace. In the few seconds that the flame stayed alight, they became aware that a man was sitting in one of the garden chairs.

Neal muttered something under his breath. Aloud, he said casually,

"Oh, hello, Charles. I thought everyone had gone."

"So it would appear," Charles replied shortly. He got up from his seat and came forward into the moonlight.

"Where's Vanessa?" Neal asked.

"She went to bed."

There was a pause. "Well . . . I suppose we'd better hit the hay too," Neal said, at length. "Is the front door locked? Are you leaving this way?"

"That's right. But there's no need for you to wait. Joanna can bolt the windows when she comes up. I want a word with her," Charles explained, without expression.

"Oh . . . oh, I see." Neal obviously didn't see, but was not inclined to query the arrangement. "Well . . . goodnight, Joanna," he said lamely.

A second later he had disappeared into the house, and she was alone with Charles.

CHAPTER FIVE

FOR several moments after Neal had left them, neither of them moved or spoke. Absurdly, Joanna found that she was trembling with apprehension.

Suddenly, realising that she was still wearing Neal's coat, she started up the terrace steps. "Neal's forgotten his jacket," she said hurriedly.

Charles stepped directly in front of her. "He won't need it in bed," he said mildly. "Let's go inside. It's chilly now, and Grandmother's windows are open."

Joanna hesitated. She wasn't sure whether it was better to stay outside where she couldn't see the expression on his face, or to go in and have lamplight revealing too much of her reactions. But it was getting cold in the open, so she moved ahead of him into the darkness of the drawing-room.

Charles drew the glass-paned doors together, lit one lamp and tipped ash in a glass tray.

"Would you like a nightcap?" he asked.

Joanna shook her head. "Look, I'm really rather sleepy. Can't this wait till the morning?" she said edgily.

Charles gave her a quizzical look. "You *are* getting adjusted quickly. In Paris, the night would still be young."

"We aren't in Paris."

"Do you wish we were?" he enquired, pouring himself a small whisky from a cut glass decanter.

"Oh, really, this is too much!" Joanna began impatiently. "I'm too tired to——"

"No, you're not. You're scared," he cut in briskly.

She gaped at him. "Scared?" she repeated blankly. "Why on earth should I be scared?"

"I'm not sure." He leaned against the arm of the sofa.

"The most obvious reason is that you're expecting some retribution for your antics earlier on."

Joanna swallowed. "If we must have a *tête-à-tête* at this hour perhaps I could have a cigarette," she said frigidly, slipping off Neal's jacket and laying it over a chair.

Charles raised his eyebrows a fraction, but he didn't comment. By a supreme effort of will, she managed to keep her hand steady as he held the lighter for her.

"Thank you," she said coolly, and sat down with her back to the light.

"Now don't say 'What antics?'" he went on. "Because you know very well what antics."

"I suppose you mean my singing—though it's not a very flattering way to refer to it," Joanna said airily. "You can hardly blame me for that, Charles. It was Neal's idea."

"But you don't deny that you were trying to shock us?"

"No, I don't deny it. Why should I? Since I've waived my fee for this visit, I feel justified in behaving as I please—within reason. I don't think it upset Grandmother."

"On the contrary, she was highly amused," he conceded.

"But you weren't, I gather?"

"I didn't say that. I thought you did the second number very well. Tell me, does your heart always speed up to that extent when you're working?"

Joanna drew carefully on the cigarette, and wondered how people could make a habit of smoking when it tasted so acrid and unpleasant. "I don't follow you."

"I took your pulse," he said mockingly. "It was phenomenal."

She flushed. "Probably because your grip was cutting off my circulation."

"Oh, surely not." He came round the end of the sofa, sat down beside her, and took hold of her hand. "It certainly isn't bruised."

With every instinct urging her to snatch her hand away and jump up, Joanna forced herself to stay motionless. What is the matter with me? she thought wildly.

"Look, I'd like to get to bed," she said at last, when

108

he seemed likely to go on studying her fingers indefinitely. "Can't you come to the point—whatever it is?"

He laid her hand gently on the cushions, and stood up. "I think you're right," he said, in an odd tone. "It is a bit late for a discussion. We'll talk about it tomorrow. You know where the switches to the staircase lights are, I suppose?"

"Oh, yes, of course," she exclaimed impatiently. "But —talk about *what*, Charles?"

He was already at the french windows. "I'll tell you— tomorrow," he said maddeningly. "Goodnight, Joanna. Sleep tight." And before she could insist on an explanation, he had moved lightly across the terrace and was out of sight.

With mingled curiosity and vexation, Joanna bolted the windows, stubbed out her wasted cigarette, and switched off the lamp. Then she felt her way carefully to the door.

There was enough moonlight in the hall for her to see the staircase without finding the switch. But as her hand touched the newel post, she heard the muted note of an engine starting up, and she paused.

What *was* it about Charles that made her so hyper-naturally sensitive to every subtle gradation of tone, every glance and gesture? She was even peculiarly aware of him when they were both talking to other people. It was as if . . . as if she had become magnetised by the man, so that whenever he was present she was struggling against a . . . what? Attraction? Oh, no—of course not! If anything, she disliked him. He was too positive, too over-bearing, too knowledgeable.

Too much a man, perhaps? The suggestion seemed to come from a small inner voice. *Wasn't that why you couldn't fall in love with Yves—because you felt a weakness in him? Yet now that you've met a man who isn't weak, you're half afraid of him?*

There was a large orb of polished mahogany topping the newel post. Joanna leaned against the post and rested her hot forehead on the cool surface of the wood. But *why* am I afraid? she thought distractedly.

Because you know what a man like Charles could do to

109

you, the voice seemed to answer. *He could steal your precious detachment, destroy all your plans and ambitions. He could make you fall in love with him.*

"No!" Her reaction was so violent that she said the word aloud, startling herself with her own voice. Her heart was thumping again, her mouth dry. He can't—I won't! she thought desperately. I don't want to fall in love, not with anyone. I don't want to be dependent.

She was half-way up the stairs when there was a rustling sound in the corridor and the landing light was switched on. Joanna stopped short, blinking. Then Mrs. Durrant appeared at the head of the staircase. She was wearing a blue wool dressing-gown and a thick mesh setting net. There was a film of night cream on her face, and without rouge and with the net stretched across her forehead she looked sallow and plain.

"You!" she exclaimed, in a taut voice. Then, sharply: "Where is Vanessa?"

Joanna climbed the rest of the stairs. "In bed, I should think. Charles said she had gone up."

"But he's only just left. I heard the car."

Joanna nodded. She was too preoccupied with her own emotions to see that there was a suppressed agitation in her aunt's manner, an almost feverish glitter about her eyes.

As Joanna moved to pass her, she shot out a hand and seized the girl's sleeve. "Why did she go to bed? What happened?" she demanded urgently.

"I suppose she was tired," Joanna said vaguely, trying to withdraw her arm. Mrs. Durrant's nails were digging through the silk.

"Of course she wasn't tired!" the older woman snapped impatiently. Her eyes narrowed and gleamed. *"You've been with him—alone!"* Her voice had a hissing note. "What were you doing down there?"

Joanna edged backwards, repelled. There were beads of moisture bursting through the skin-food on her aunt's nose and chin, and her nostrils were dilated and quivering.

"We weren't doing anything," she said helplessly. "I'd been in the garden with Neal, and then Charles said he wanted to speak to me."

110

"What about?"

"I don't know yet. It was later than he'd realised, so he said he'd leave it till tomorrow. Hadn't we better go to bed, Aunt Monica? It must be nearly two o'clock."

For one instant, Mrs. Durrant looked so wild and venomous that Joanna expected her to strike her. Then, with a visible effort of will, the woman regained control of herself. She still looked angry and hostile, but her voice, when she spoke, no longer had the rising note of hysteria.

"I hope you haven't disturbed Mother, coming up at this hour," she said frigidly. "This evening was sufficiently taxing for her without your waking her up." And, with that, she wheeled round and disappeared into her room again, leaving Joanna to turn out the lights and go to her own bed in an even more troubled frame of mind.

*   *   *

She was roused the next morning by an insistent tapping on her door. A quick glance at her wristwatch showed that it was nearing quarter to eleven, and with an exclamation of dismay she tumbled out of bed and shrugged on her nylon housecoat.

Opening the door, she found it was Neal who had woken her.

"Sorry if I broke up a good dream," he said cheerfully. "But it's such a marvellous day, I thought we might run over to the coast for a quick bathe. It's only fifteen miles, so we can easily be back by lunch-time. The others have all gone to church."

Joanna pushed back her tumbled hair and blinked. It had been almost dawn before she had finally closed her eyes, and then to sleep only shallowly.

"Oh, Neal, I don't think so," she said wearily. "I feel like death, and anyway I haven't got a swimsuit with me."

"Borrow one of Van's," he suggested.

"No, I couldn't do that—not without asking her first. To be honest, the most I feel up to is a quiet sunbathe in the garden."

"Okay, we'll bask together. Maybe you'll feel more lively after lunch," he agreed equably. "I say, do you always lock yourself in at night?"

111

Until he mentioned it, Joanna had forgotten that she had locked her door the night before. And, just now, she had been too dismayed at having overslept to be aware of having to unlock it again.

Now, as she remembered the reason for such an unusual precaution, a wave of embarrassed colour suffused her face. "No, not usually," she admitted. "I—I must have done it absent-mindedly."

Her flush and the hint of a stammer made Neal look faintly perplexed. But he made no comment.

"Well, I'll get Alice to rustle up some toast and coffee for you. See you downstairs."

"Neal—" Joanna hesitated, biting her lip. "Look, why don't you have that bathe?" she said, managing a smile. "As a matter of fact, I've several letters to write, so I could do with a couple of hours alone."

He stared at her searchingly for a moment, then shrugged his shoulders. "Oh, all right, if you don't want me around," he answered shortly. And before she could protest, he had gone off down the corridor.

After she had washed, Joanna put on a sun-top and yellow shorts. She would change into a dress before the others got back from morning service, but in the meantime, shorts were more relaxing—and she certainly needed relaxation at the moment.

Leaving the bedroom, she caught sight of the door-key again and made a wry grimace. It seemed silly now, but last night's scene with her aunt had left her nerves jangling. Long after she had climbed into bed, she hadn't been able to dispel the memory of the malevolent expression which had momentarily contorted Mrs. Durrant's features. And when a board had creaked in the passage, she had been convinced that someone was skulking in the darkness. Nonsense, of course, but then everyone's imagination tended to work overtime in the still small hours. Anyway, she had had to lock the door before she could attempt to drop off.

Neal had gone when she went downstairs, and she had a snack breakfast in the kitchen with Alice. Then, with her writing case and the Sunday papers at her elbow, she settled down for a peaceful hour on the terrace.

112

After ten minutes in the sun, with the scent of roses drifting on the light breeze and the sound of somebody's lawn mower coming from a distance, her eyelids began to droop. Lying full length on the comfortable wicker garden couch, she let herself drift off to sleep.

When she woke up, Charles was sitting nearby with a tall glass of lager in his hand.

"Oh, heavens, what time it is? I've got to change," Joanna exclaimed in alarm. She felt as if she had been asleep for hours.

"No hurry, it's only just twelve. The others won't be back for an hour yet. They're calling on some friends after church," Charles said easily.

Joanna sat up and smoothed her hair. She wondered how long he had been there, and wished she had a shirt to slip over the scanty sun-top.

But, whatever he had done while she was asleep, Charles was not looking at her now. His dark head was resting against the back of his chair and he was looking up over the tree-tops that screened the bottom of the garden.

"I thought you'd be out with Neal," he said casually, after a silence of several minutes.

"He's gone to the coast for a swim. I felt more like lazing." There was a jug of iced fruit cup on the table now, Joanna discovered. She poured some into a tumbler and jostled the ice-chips for a moment.

"Was the inertia genuine or strategic?" Charles asked lazily.

"Genuine, of course. I didn't sleep too well."

He turned his head and looked at her. "You could have decided to give him a mild set-down."

"Why should I do that? I like Neal—very much."

"I gathered that last night," Charles said drily. He lit a cigarette. "Were you going to let him kiss you??"

Joanna drew in a breath. "I don't know what you mean," she said flatly.

He sighed. "Look, Joanna, this ploy of hen-witted innocence is wearing pretty thin. You're mulish and sometimes misguided—but you aren't stupid."

113

"Perhaps you'd prefer it if I told you to mind your own business," she retorted sharply.

He laughed. "Why not, if that's what you mean? But, in this case, it is my business."

"I'd certainly like to know how you work that out," she said acidly. "Since we're both over eighteen and free agents, whether we kiss or don't kiss seems to be up to us."

"Did you want him to kiss you?" he asked, in an odd tone.

She forced herself to speak casually. "Not specially. But I don't take the view that a kiss must have some tremendous significance. It's often just . . . something enpoyable."

Charles didn't reply at once.

After a moment, he got up and strolled to the other end of the terrace, then back again. Whatever he was thinking, it was not reflected in his face.

Suddenly, pushing her feet further over, he sat on the end of the lounger. "Don't let Neal's fecklessness mislead you, Joanna," he said abruptly. "Under that gay play-boy manner he affects, he's pretty emotional."

Joanna sipped her drink. "While you, Cousin Charles," she said sweetly, "are so superhuman that you have no emotions at all."

Charles's eyes narrowed. "Is that meant to crush my ego—or could it be a challenge?" he enquired softly.

Joanna gasped. "Why, of all the conceited, arrogant——!" she began.

He flipped his cigarette into the flower-bed and leaned towards her, his hands gripping the wicker arms of the lounger.

Instinctively, Joanna shrank back against the cushions.

"You surprise me, Cousin Joanna," he said softly, silkily. "I wouldn't have thought you were the type to panic."

Joanna swallowed. "You've an odd sense of humour," she said coldly. "I'm afraid I'm not amused." But although her chin had come up, and she met his eyes, her heart was thudding.

Charles bent a fraction closer. "What makes you think

114

I'm joking? I may not be as susceptible as young Neal, but I'm not entirely immune to a pretty face. And, as you said just now, a kiss needn't change a relationship. Let's just . . . enjoy ourselves." His hands shifted to her elbows and drew her towards him.

"Please, Charles—stop baiting me," she said, in a stifled voice.

His eyes mocked her. "You don't have to be coy, sweetheart."

Her fists clenched. "I'm *not* being coy," she flared hotly. "Will you let me go!"

"Why? Is my touch so repugnant to you?"

Joanna set her teeth. Then, so suddenly that she fell back against the cushions again, Charles let her go. His ears, sharper than hers, must have heard a footfall in the drawing-room. When Alice came through the french windows, he was standing up, finishing his lager.

"Will you be staying to lunch, Mr. Charles?" the maid enquired.

"No, thanks, Alice. But I wouldn't mind another glass of this if you've got some on ice," he said casually.

After she had gone, he lit another cigarette. "I'm sorry about that, Joanna," he said briefly. "I suppose it was unfair to bait you. But at least it proved my theory."

An apology—even if it wasn't made in a particularly penitent tone—was the last thing Joanna had expected.

"Oh, really? What theory?" she asked stiffly.

"That, under the veneer of sophistication, you're a good deal less self-possessed than you'd admit."

Joanna examined her nails. "Perhaps I am," she conceded lightly. "But I don't think your . . . experiment was very conclusive. I'm fairly used to that sort of behaviour from other men, but I naturally didn't expect a pass from you."

His mouth twitched. "It was hardly a pass, d'you think? But anyway, why not from me?"

Joanna floundered for a moment. "Well . . . you just don't seem that type," she said awkwardly.

115

"What type?"

"Oh, heavens, must we discuss it?" she exclaimed, on an exasperated note.

"It might teach you something you don't appear to know," he replied mildly. "Most men are 'that type,' my girl. It's their motives and approach which vary. And even when you're dealing with a proverbially phlegmatic Englishman, you can't just fling out a challenge without getting some reaction," he added sardonically.

Joanna opened her mouth to deny that she had meant to challenge him. But she had an uncomfortable feeling that he was right, that she had wanted to spark some reaction.

She changed tack. "Aren't you taking a good deal for granted?" she asked crisply. "Or is it inconceivable that any girl should be immune to the fatal Carlyon charm?".

He laughed. "A woman doesn't have to be attracted to a man to want to prove to herself that she has some effect on him. Throwing out lures is a basic feminine instinct."

"Well, at least you concede that you can't dazzle our entire sex," Joanna said negligently. "But I wouldn't rely too heavily on that odd bit of amateur psychology, if I were you. The women in Merefield may be like that, but it isn't universal."

A car approached the house and she got to her feet. "I must change."

"Don't forget we have a date tonight," Charles called, as she reached the french windows.

Joanna looked blank.

"The Drurys invited us to supper, remember? I'll pick you up about seven. No need to dress up." Even at twenty paces she could see the glint of devilment in his eyes. "And afterwards we'll have a nightcap at my place, and I'll show you my . . . record collection," he tacked on blandly.

*　　　　*　　　　*

Joanna spent the afternoon talking to her grandmother. Neal had not come in for lunch and she could not help feeling that he was behaving rather childishly, and that there might be an element of truth in Charles's warning to her.

116

Cathy and Vanessa were playing tennis at a house down the road, and Mrs. Durrant had gone out to tea, so Joanna and Mrs. Carlyon had theirs in the shelter of the arbour.

"Monica doesn't like eating in the open, but I think it's rather fun," Mrs. Carlyon said gaily, after Alice had brought out the big silver tray with its load of pretty china and covered silver warming-dishes.

Eating a hot buttered scone while the old lady adjusted the little three-legged spirit burner, Joanna thought that the relationship between her grandmother and her aunt was more like that of a mischievous little girl and her disciplinarian governess.

"Mm . . . these are delicious," she said presently, biting into a wafer-thin cucumber sandwich.

"Yes, Monica is an excellent housekeeper—much better than I ever was," Mrs. Carlyon said warmly, as if feeling that her earlier remark might have been slightly disloyal. "She does all the cooking, you know. Alice only serves our meals. It takes her all her time to keep the house in order, poor dear. Considering what a barn of a place it is, we're lucky she stays with us."

"I didn't realise Aunt Monica cooked everything," Joanna remarked.

"Oh yes, dear. She even insists on making this wholemeal bread—and I must agree it is much nicer than those insipid steam-baked lumps that the bakeries turn out nowadays. It's a pity in a way that she didn't take up domestic science when she was a girl. I sometimes think she would have been happier with a career. But of course your grandfather didn't approve of girls going out to work, so she married poor Edward Durrant. A nice man, but rather a weak character. Monica needed someone who would stand up to her—someone like Charles."

"You're very fond of him, aren't you?" Joanna said, smiling.

Mrs. Carlyon nodded. "I know one shouldn't have favourites," she admitted. "But Charles has always been especially dear to me. Perhaps it's because he is so much like your grandfather—but without John's hardness and moodiness." She smiled to herself. "You know, when I was very young I used to wonder what kept old people

117

alive. I couldn't see any point in going on when one was past all the exciting things in life . . . falling in love and marrying and having babies. I expect you've wondered that, haven't you?"

Joanna hesitated, and before she could answer her grandmother patted her hand. "Yes, of course you have," she said, chuckling. "At your age, anyone over fifty seems a decrepit old fossil. But don't ever be afraid of growing old, Joanna. It isn't as depressing as it seems from a distance, you know. There are compensations. In fact, looking back on all the heartaches and uncertainties of youth, old age feels rather pleasant. One can still take a share in the young people's excitements, but one doesn't fret about the disasters. One knows from experience that no trouble lasts for ever. There's only one thing that I would like to happen before I die—and that is for Charles to marry." She paused to sip her tea. "I was afraid it might be too late for me," she said, more to herself than to Joanna. "But now . . . now I think I shall have that one last wish."

Joanna finished eating a raspberry conserve, but suddenly the feather-light sponge and pastry had less taste than sawdust. Perhaps her grandmother had also been expecting Charles to propose to Vanessa last night. Perhaps, when he had failed to do so, she had spoken to him about it. For unless he had confided to her that he did want to marry Vanessa, why should she sound so confident that her wish would soon be fulfilled?

I suppose this morning's little exercise was in the nature of a final fling, Joanna thought furiously. Well, just try it again, Cousin Charles—I'll give you a positive reaction!

*   *   *

It must have been about five o'clock, and the others were not yet home, when Joanna realised that her grandmother was breathing in a queer way. Soon after tea, Mrs. Carlyon had fallen into a doze and, to take her mind off certain unanswerable questions, Joanna had written to Gustave.

She had just sealed the envelope when she became aware that her grandmother was breathing in a series of gasps. Looking up, she was alarmed to see that the old lady was gripping the arms of her chair and seemed to be struggling to speak.

"Grandmother! What is it?" she cried anxiously.

"M-my tablets . . . in . . . in bag." The words were scarcely coherent.

Joanna scrabbled in the big tapestry needlework bag beneath the old lady's chair, found the small white chemist's box, read the instructions and poured some of the now tepid water from the kettle. Surprisingly, her hands were perfectly steady although, inwardly, she was panic-stricken. Ought she to race into the house and telephone a doctor? No, she couldn't leave the old lady alone.

Please God, make the tablets work. Don't let her die. Not yet!

Ten minues later, still rather blue about the lips but quite calm and cheerful, Mrs. Carlyon was berating herself for giving Joanna such a fright.

"Don't look so anxious, dear. It was only one of my silly little attacks. They aren't nearly as bad as they look," she insisted.

But Joanna was intensely relieved when she had helped her grandmother to walk slowly back to the house and made her comfortable on the sofa. However, Mrs. Carlyon refused to allow her to call the doctor, saying that there was nothing he could do, beyond advising her to rest, and she had no intention of disturbing the poor man's Sunday without a good reason. She also made Joanna promise not to mention the incident to her aunt.

"Monica does fuss so, dear, and it doesn't do the least good. If one has my complaint, one must learn to accept these little upsets from time to time. It's no use making a to-do about it."

Nevertheless Joanna was impatient for Mrs. Durrant's return, and only relaxed when she heard her aunt's voice in the hall.

*   *   *

Dick and Margaret Drury lived in one of a long row of terraced Edwardian villas. But while most of its neighbours had drab front doors and potted plants or panting plaster Alsatians between the lace curtains, No. 17 had a vivid yellow door and white plastic blinds at the windows.

These were necessary, Margaret told Joanna, because the front garden was the size of a small tablecloth and the Drurys did not reserve their "front room" for special occasions. So, without the blinds, any curious passer-by would be able to note their activities.

"Not that we have anything to hide, but it makes one feel rather like a goldfish," Margaret explained.

In spite of the inconvenience of having a front door that led straight into the sitting-room, no bathroom, and a kitchen too tiny to take a refrigerator or any other labour-saving devices, the Drurys had managed to make their little house uncommonly cosy and attractive.

"Oh, I'd like one of those stainless steel kitchens and a glossy bathroom as much as the next woman," Margaret admitted, as she showed Joanna the two cramped bedrooms, and the even smaller box-room where Bunter lay sprawled in his cot. "But there's plenty of time for Gracious Living later, and this is at least ours. We spent the first year of our marriage in a furnished flat—and that was absolute hell!"

"I think it's a dear little house," Joanna said sincerely. "I suppose the only real drawback is that there won't be much room for Bunter to roam when he starts walking. Or have you a bigger garden at the back?"

"No—only a rather squalid yard, all dustbins and drains," Margaret said wryly. "But Charles insists that I use his garden. He lives on the other side of the factory recreation ground, it's about ten minutes' walk. So whenever I long for a bit of greenery, I push Bunter round there and he can crawl all over the place." She grinned. "I must admit I do feel rather envious when we spend an evening with Charles. His house is bliss, not a bit the typical bachelor establishment. Have you been there yet?"

Joanna shook her head. She didn't want to discuss Charles, so she changed the subject by asking more about Bunter.

After supper, the two men washed up and then they all played rummy. Joanna saw Charles flicker a glance at her when Dick suggested the game. Perhaps he thought she might have a phobia about cards because of her father. But there wasn't much relation between a hilarious game

120

of rummy and the high-stake poker by which Michael had made his living, she thought.

Although she did her best to ignore Charles—at least in the sense of not looking at him except when he spoke to her, and not speaking to him more than was necessary to preserve an appearance of normality—it was not easy. Dick and Margaret were both on the short side and slightly built. But Charles's height and breadth of shoulder were doubly noticeable in such a tiny house. He had to dip his head to get through the doorways, and his long legs seemed to stretch halfway across the room.

Once, when they were sitting next to each other at the supper table, his knee had brushed against hers. "Sorry," he had said briefly, and she knew it had been accidental, but even that trivial contact made her pulses quicken.

Towards ten o'clock, there were plaintive wails from upstairs. Dick and Margaret groaned.

"Bunter's been waking up every night since his teeth started coming," Margaret said, with a sigh. "He bawls the place down for half an hour and then drops off again. I'm afraid I'll have to bring him downstairs. It's all against the rules, but we've found it's the only way. Otherwise he'd go on yelling all night. Make some coffee, will you, darling?" she added to her husband.

Glimpsed in his cot, Bunter Drury had looked a cherubic infant. But when Margaret carried him downstairs he was purple with pain and anger, and glared tearfully round the room. It wasn't until he spotted the shiny silver beads that Joanna was wearing with her grey denim dress that his bellows subsided and a gleam of interest lit his eye. Leaning perilously over his mother's arm, he reached out to touch them.

"May he play with them if I take them off?" Joanna asked.

"Oh, no—he'll break them," Margaret said anxiously.

"I don't think so. They're on a specially strong thread." But before she could unclasp the catch, Bunter had wrestled out of Margaret's grasp and scrambled along the couch. Leaning over the arm-rest, he reached up to tug at the necklace.

"Good lord! That's unusual," Dick remarked, coming back with the coffee to find his son ensconced on Joanna's lap and happily examining the the beads. "Normally he's pretty leery of strangers."

"Perhaps Joanna has that special something which attracts small children and animals," Charles remarked negligently.

Joanna's mouth hardened. Ordinarily she didn't pay much attention to babies and toddlers. But there was something oddly touching about Bunter's plump form encased in a blue and white sleeping-suit, and the confiding way he leaned against her arm. His little button nose and fat pink hands moved her to sudden tenderness. Now Charles had spoilt that feeling. He spoke as if she were putting on an act, had consciously adopted a maternal pose with the child.

The baby must have felt her stiffen. He looked up, spotted her silver ear-studs and made a grab at them. His thumb-nail, catching her cheek, left a long scratch.

"Oh, Bunter, now look what you've done!" Margaret expostulated. She snatched him off Joanna's knee and dumped him on the couch. "I'm terribly sorry, Joanna. I ought not to have let him loose on you. He's always gouging holes in people."

"It's hardly a mortal wound," Joanna said, laughing. "Don't look so horrified, Margaret."

"It's bleeding. I'll get you a tissue." Margaret dived into a cupboard and produced a box of Kleenex.

"You can't wonder the kid injures people. Look at the length of his nails," Dick remarked, retrieving Joanna's beads from his erring child.

"Yes, I know—but it's so terribly difficult to cut them," Margaret explained. "Usually I do them when he's asleep, but now the least touch wakes him up. I'll get you some antiseptic," she added to Joanna. "I really am frightfully sorry."

"Oh, calm down, Maggie. The girl isn't bleeding to death," Charles said lightly.

He took a tissue from the box, tipped up Joanna's chin and blotted her cheek. "It won't mar your beauty for more than a couple of days," he told her casually.

122

The touch of his fingers was like an electric contact. Joanna bore it for five seconds, then jerked away. "I can deal with it," she said tautly.

Charles had his back to the others and, for one instant, there was such a fierce glint in his eyes that she caught her breath. But it was only a momentary reaction and, in the space of a heart-beat, his face was impassive again.

After a drink of orange juice and a cuddle with his father, Bunter grew drowsy again. Soon after he had been put back to bed, Charles said they must be going.

"The party went on pretty late last night, so we could do with some extra sleep," he explained, when Margaret protested that it was barely ten.

"Oh, yes, I was forgetting," she agreed. She smiled at Joanna, still remorseful about the scratch. "Once you have a baby, it's like being Cinderella," she said. "You always have to be home on the stroke of midnight or you get blacklisted by the baby-sitters' union."

In view of Charles' remark, Joanna expected him to take her straight back to Mere House. Neither of them spoke as they drove away from Connaught Street, and in spite of the warmth of the evening, the atmosphere in the car was decidedly chilly.

It wasn't until they turned into an unfamiliar gateway, and Joanna realised that he was carrying out his original intention that she broke the silence.

"I thought we were going to have an early night."

Charles brought the car to a standstill outside the grey-bricked Georgian house. "Another half an hour won't hurt us." He swung out on to the drive, strolled round the bonnet and opened her door.

Joanna didn't move.

"All the same, I don't think I'll come in this evening, thanks."

He said nothing, but continued to hold the door for her. After a few moments' pause, when she realised that he was quite capable of standing there indefinitely, she made an exasperated sound and slid out of the car.

The front door was unlatched and led into a small black and white tiled hallway with a white-painted staircase

123

curving up to the first floor. The walls were papered with silver and white Regency stripes and there was a bowl of dark red roses on an elegant Sheraton console.

"If you'd like to powder, the bathroom is the first door on the landing."

"No, thank you," Joanna said ungraciously.

In spite of her intention to be markedly offhand, she couldn't repress a murmur of appreciation when he showed her into the sitting-room. It was long and narrow with two tall windows facing south-west so that the last lingering rose and gold streaks of the late summer sunset could be seen through the upper panes. Pale green damask curtains and darker velvet squabs on the window-seats contrasted with the bleached pine of the inside shutters.

The central furnishings were a skilful blend of graceful antiques and well designed modern pieces. There were two long four-seater sofas, one covered with silver-grey corduroy, the other with a pale tweedy fabric. The carpet was a thick close-fitted Wilton in a subtle shade of greige, and the lamp-fittings were probably Scandinavian. But one of the coffee tables was a graceful rosewood period piece, and there was a huge gilded looking-glass and a hanging cabinet filled with old porcelain on the end wall. It was the kind of room, Joanna thought immediately, which suited every mood. It would make a perfect background for formal entertainment, yet one could also relax here.

"Do you like it?" Charles asked, from close behind.

Joanna jumped slightly. She hadn't been aware of it, but she must have been standing inside the doorway and taking in every detail for at least two minutes.

"Oh, yes—it's a lovely room," she said warmly, momentarily forgetting her intended stiffness.

There was a modern metal cocktail trolley standing just inside the door. Charles pushed it towards one of the window seats and removed the napkins which had covered some plates of canapés.

"Come and sit down," he invited, tossing an extra cushion against one end of the seat and gesturing for her to sit there.

Joanna did so, and accepted a glass of sherry. There were some miniature vol-au-vents in a heated dish, his housekeeper's speciality, Charles explained. The crisp puff pastry cases were filled with a delicious spiced shrimp paté.

"You know," Charles said suddenly, "I've only just realised it, but this room might have been designed for someone with your colouring. That remarkable hair is the perfect finishing touch."

He had never spoken to her in quite that tone before, and a quiver ran down her spine.

"Do you think so?" she answered lightly. Then, smoothing her pleated skirt, "But I don't think grey denim fits in very well. A room like this calls for chiffon . . . something more feminine."

"It isn't clothes that make a woman feminine," he said drily.

Joanna looked out into the garden. "I should have thought clothes were sixty per cent of it."

The last light was fading from the sky and a pale yellow moon hung over the dark mass of treetops. She began to count the stars—it would distract her from being so aware of him.

"I don't agree," Charles said amiably. "I've seen girls in overalls and gumboots who looked far more feminine than other girls in full glamour rig."

"Well, if clothes have nothing to do with it, how would you define a really feminine woman?" Joanna asked curiously. Star-counting was not, she discovered, at all effective.

She had replaced her glass on the trolley, and Charles refilled it. He opened his cigarette case, changed his mind and slipped it back in his pocket.

"I'm not sure that one can define these things," he said slowly. "It's the senses they affect, not the intellect. I suppose the nearest definition might be a woman who makes a man feel more manly. Or maybe a woman who enjoys being a woman. Some women—and they aren't all tweedy types—seem almost to resent their own sex. Take your aunt, for example. She's superficially feminine, but I think she'd have been a much happier person if she'd been born a male. She has aggressive instincts, and a feminine woman hasn't."

"I must be unfeminine too. I often have some very aggressive instincts," Joanna said carelessly. "I wonder if you've ever considered what it's like to *be* a woman, Charles. Oh, I know we're supposed to have equal opportunities and equal status nowadays. But it isn't really true, you know. We're only equal to men until we marry them. Then instead of being individuals, we're wives and mothers. Whatever else we may want to do with our lives has to be fitted in between running a house and minding children. Even if a woman has genius, it can rarely survive that inevitable division of energy."

It was completely dark now, so she could not see his expression. He was probably laughing at her for the sudden outburst of speechifying, she thought with a flicker of resentment.

But Charles didn't sound amused when he answered her. "But isn't it worth it, on the whole?" he asked quietly.

Joanna wished he would switch on one of the lamps. Sitting in the dark was beginning to make her feel edgy.

"How should I know? I haven't tried marriage yet," she said flippantly. "And anyway, I'm not the romantic type."

"I don't think you know what you are—and you're afraid of finding out."

He moved suddenly, and before she could check herself, Joanna had jumped to her feet and darted out of reach. There was a muffled clink as her skirt brushed against the trolley and the tinkle of breaking glass. As a lamp illumined the room, she saw that her sherry glass—a fragile piece of crystal—had been swept to the floor. Pieces were scattered on the carpet and wine was soaking into the pile.

Mute with embarrassment—for it was obvious that he had leaned forward only to turn on the light—she stood biting her lip while Charles mopped the stain with his handkerchief and picked up the fragments.

"Oh, dear, I'm so sorry," she stammered. "Let me get a cloth. If—if it isn't sponged, the sherry will leave a mark."

He tipped a palmful of shards into an ash-tray. "Don't worry. Mrs. Howard will deal with it while I'm running you home."

And before she could offer some halting excuse for her

clumsiness, he had stepped past her and gone off to speak to his housekeeper. He was away about three minutes, and when he came back his face was completely unreadable.

"Shall we go?" he said formally.

As soon as the car was in motion, he switched on the radio. Still hot with chagrin, Joanna listened dully to the end of a news bulletin and the beginning of a record programme. But what the news had been, or what disc was topping the charts, she had no idea.

Back at Mere House, she waited for him to shut off the music and said again, "I really am frightfully sorry about——"

"Good lord, it was only a glass," he cut in briskly. Then, after getting out and coming round to her side, "Anyway, it isn't that you should be so upset about."

She slid off the seat and straightened. "What else?" she said warily.

Charles closed the door and moved towards the house. "All this flinching and fencing is beginning to make me feel like a satyr," he said lightly.

They were under the portico now, and his hand was at the latch.

"You don't understand . . ." she began.

"Don't I?" His hands gripped her shoulders and he pulled her against him.

For one shattering moment she was powerless to move. But his kiss, when it came, as as swift as her own heart-beats, and lighter than a feather touch. His lips just glanced over her cheek, and then she was free again.

"There!" he said mockingly. "Now at least you know the worst. It wasn't so terrible, was it?"

Seconds later, the car was speeding down the drive.

*　　　*　　　*

There had been two previous occasions when, overnight, Joanna's whole life had changed course. The first had been realising how her father was getting his living. The second had been Michael's death.

Now, waking up on Monday morning in the bedroom at Mere House, she was instantly aware that, once again,

127

something cataclysmic had happened. Yet for several moments she couldn't remember what it was.

Then it hit her. *I'm in love with Charles Carlyon.* With a stifled groan she buried her head in the pillow.

But disaster, she knew from experience, was never mended by giving way to despair. Sooner or later one had to brace up and deal with it—and there was certainly no question about the best way to deal with this one. She had to leave Merefield. At once.

She had washed and dressed, and had even got as far as taking her suitcase out of the corner cupboard, when she realised that the issue was not as clear-cut as she had thought. There was her grandmother to consider. She couldn't walk out of the house at a moment's notice and without explanation. It might bring on another of Mrs. Carlyon's attacks. Yet what explanation was there? And every moment's delay could only worsen the situation.

A tape at the door made her catch her breath and hastily shove the case under the bed. It was Cathy.

"Are you up?—Oh, yes. I say Joanna, Gran has given me twenty pounds to buy some holiday clothes. Isn't she a lamb! If you're not doing anything this morning, I wondered if you'd come and help me choose? Imagine—twenty pounds!"

Joanna hesitated. Then she said brightly, "What riches! Of course I'll come with you, Cathy."

All through breakfast, her mind was working on the problem of how to leave Merefield without upsetting her grandmother. Finally, she decided to telephone Gustave again. She would get him to write to her, putting forward the date on which rehearsals for her London opening were to begin. In the meantime she would tell Mrs. Carlyon about the new contract and thus pave the way for a reluctant but unavoidable departure. Her grandmother would understand. She would probably be quite excited. The only hazard was getting through the next four or five days without seeing Charles. Still, he would be back at the factory this week, so it might be managed. And, once she was in London and working again . . .

But an hour later, as they caught a bus to the shopping centre and Cathy chattered excitedly about the best way to budget her unexpected windfall, Joanna was beginning to have second thoughts.

Just before they had left the house, she had been standing on the landing, checking the contents of her bag, when she had overheard the end of an argument which was taking place in the hallway below her.

"Well, I think you're being jolly disloyal," Vanessa's voice had said sharply. "You know Mother doesn't like her, but you deliberately fawn all over her."

"Oh, don't be such an ass, Van. It's not fawning to ask someone to go shopping with you. You're always telling me I don't plan my clothes properly. If Joanna helps me, I shan't make any mistakes. Even you must admit that she's got marvellous taste."

"That isn't the point."

"Well, what *is* the point, then?" Cathy had asked reasonably. "Just because you and Ma don't like her—and we all know why *that* is—I can't see any reason why Neal and I should be horrid to her."

"What do you mean—'we all know why that is'?" Vanessa demanded coldly.

"Anyone could see that you were green when Charles took her out last night. He's never taken you to a meal with the Drurys, has he? It's really rather odd, when one comes to think of it. I mean, they're two of his closest friends, and if he was seriously thinking of marrying you——"

Cathy's words ended with an audible gasp, followed by the sound of a stinging slap.

"Why, you little beast! How dare——" But Vanessa also stopped short, because the kitchen door had opened and Alice had evidently appeared.

It was only then that Joanna had realised she was eavesdropping, and had quickly gone back to her bedroom. And by the time she had gone downstairs, Vanessa had disappeared and there was not even a lingering redness mark on Cathy's cheek to betray what had taken place.

Not that the slap had been particularly unexpected, Joanna thought, as the bus stopped at some traffic lights. Disliking her as they did, it was obvious that both Mrs.

129

Durrant and her elder daughter would censure Cathy's friendliness.

But somehow overhearing the quarrel had given her a fresh slant on the situation. Ever since her arrival, she realised suddenly, she had been mentally linking Charles and Vanessa together. Not because they showed signs of being in love, but because, in superficial terms, they had seemed so well matched. Now, viewing their characters more analytically, she began to have doubts. Why *should* Charles want to marry Vanessa? She was pretty and palpably available—but what else? She certainly wasn't bright, or even amusing. And far from being sensually exciting, she gave the impression that passionate emotions would embarrass her. If all Charles wanted was a presentable domesticated girl who could be relied on to fit into his life with the minimum of disturbance—why, yes, Vanessa would fill the bill very adequately. But since all his creature comforts were already well supplied, it seemed rather an unnecessary alliance. Moreover, if Charles *did* want Vanessa, why was he delaying? He was the type who, having made a decision, acts on it.

I don't believe he cares a button for her, Joanna thought abruptly, and with an unbidden upsurge of relief. But even if he isn't interested in her, it doesn't mean . . .

"Joanna, you aren't listening," Cathy accused. "I don't believe you've heard a word I've said."

Joanna pulled herself together. "Sorry, Cathy, I was day-dreaming," she apologised.

But although she could easily have invented an excuse to go off on her own for half an hour and make the call to Gustave Hugo, she didn't do so. Knowing she was being a fool, yet suddenly reckless, she had decided to stay on in Merefield and take whatever came to her.

For three days, Charles didn't come to Mere House at all. On Friday afternoon, aching yet dreading to see him again, Joanna couldn't stand the suspense any longer. Although the hot spell had given place to sullen skies and intermittent rain, she put on a raincoat and headscarf and went out for a walk. When the rain began to fall more heavily and was beginning to soak through her coat, she ducked into a cinema and spent a couple of hours trying to concentrate on the more dramatic dilemma of a girl whose lover might be a murderer.

It was after seven o'clock when she caught a homeward bus. However, it was unlikely that anyone had missed her as they had all gone out to tea, and Mrs. Durrant had said that dinner would be an hour late.

Back at the house, she hung her coat on a peg, untied the scarf and combed her hair. There were voices coming from the drawing-room, so instead of going straight upstairs to change her shoes, she went to tell them she was back—just in case her grandmother might be getting anxious.

Even before she opened the door, she had a premonition that Charles was in the room—and she was right. He was standing by the window with his back to her, and the sight of his well-shaped dark head after three endless days of waiting sent a pang of delight through her.

The next thing she noticed was that Neal was at home—although he had said at breakfast that he would not be back until late. He and Cathy were sitting side by side on the couch, while Vanessa stood beside the big armchair, her hand on her mother's shoulder. They were all of them staring at Joanna with curious fixity.

"So you're back." Mrs. Durrant sounded slightly hoarse, as if she were starting a cold. "Where have you been?"

"I went to the pictures. I hope you haven't——" Joanna began. She stopped short at the baleful glitter in her aunt's eyes. The older woman was glaring at her with the same undisguised enmity that she had shown the other night on the landing. "I'm sorry, Aunt Monica," she started again. "It was raining so hard that I——"

"*Sorry!*" Monica Durrant spat out the single exclamation as it it were an obscene word.

And it was then, with her aunt regarding her with cold loathing, and the others as motionless and mute as figures in a tableau, that Joanna was gripped by another and more agonising presentiment. Where was her grandmother?

It was Cathy who answered her unspoken question. "Gran's dead," she whispered huskily. "She . . . she died this afternoon."

For a moment, Joanna couldn't take it in. It simply

131

wasn't possible that in the space of a few hours . . . Her mind reeled from the shock.

"No!" she breathed helplessly. "Oh . . . *no!*"

Suddenly Mrs. Durrant sprang to her feet. "Yes, she's dead!" she cried raspingly. "And it's your fault . . . your fault, do you hear? You should never have come here."

"Monica!" Charles had swung round from the window.

But neither his warning tone nor Vanessa's restraining hand could halt Mrs. Durrant now. The last remnants of control had slipped from her, and she was shaking like someone in a fever, tears pouring down her face, her mouth twitching uncontrollably. But it was not grief and pain that tormented her. It was hatred—stark bitter hatred.

"Well, it's true, isn't it?" she demanded of them. "Of course it's true. If *she* hadn't come here, Mother might have lived for years. But all this fuss and upset was too much for her. She wanted to forget the past—not relive it."

"Mother, please——!" Neal was on his feet now. But his agonised interjection only fanned Mrs. Durrant's wrath.

"Don't you dare take her part, you stupid boy!" She was almost screaming at him. "You're just like your wretched father. Some cheap little siren smiles at you and you're half besotted. D'you think I haven't seen the way you look at her . . . and you too, Charles. All men are the same! A pretty face, a provocative figure . . . and you've no more judgment than a fly. But I'm not deceived—oh, no! I see through her scheming ways. She doesn't charm me!"

"Mummy, don't!" Now it was Cathy who attempted to stem the torrent—Cathy, looking ashen and terrified.

"She's just like her mother," Mrs. Durrant stormed. "She's Nina all over again. Just because she's pretty and artful and grasping, she doesn't care who she hurts. That's how Nina was, and that's how *she* is. I hated Nina, and I hate her too. I hate her, do you hear? *I hate her!*"

It was over as suddenly as it had started. As abruptly as she had jumped to her feet, Mrs. Durrant collapsed into a chair. She didn't weep or have hysterics, she just lay there panting and exhausted.

For several moments nobody moved. Even Vanessa was too shocked to be capable of action.

Joanna, too, was stunned. The tirade had swept over her like some immense tidal wave. She had seen it coming, held her breath and, miraculously, survived. The actual words . . . the bitter denunciation, were all jumbled together in her head. But one thing was clear: that first cruel indictment—'*It's your fault . . . your fault.*'

No! she thought numbly. No—please . . .

Vanessa was the first to recover. Hurrying forward, she knelt by her mother's chair and began anxiously to chafe the lax hands and murmur soothing words.

Joanna watched her for a moment. Then, slowly, she looked at Neal and Cathy. They couldn't believe it was her fault—surely they couldn't?

But after meeting her eyes for a second, they both looked quickly away. They didn't move physically, but she had a horrible conviction that, inwardly, they were shrinking away from her.

Finally, hardly daring to turn her head, she looked at Charles. He was standing behind the couch, his hands gripping the backrest so violently that every vein and sinew stood out from the taut flesh. And although he did not turn away as she looked her mute appeal, his face was set in a mask of implacable anger. His eyes were like chips of flint.

With a stifled groan, Joanna turned and fled. Snatching up her coat, half blinded by stinging tears, she tore open the front door and almost fell down the steps. Then she ran and ran until her heart seemed threatening to burst.

CHAPTER SIX

IT was after ten o'clock when Joanna realised that she could not trudge aimlessly about the streets for much longer. Her feet were aching, her clothes sodden, her whole body chilled and spent. But she couldn't go back to Mere House—not tonight, or ever again.

She had never felt so solitary and wretched in her life, not even after Michael had died. In Paris, even when it rained, there were always the lighted windows of the cafés and *bistros,* and the savoury aromas from back-street *épiceries* to cheer one's loneliness.

But, in Merefield, the stores closed sharp at half-past five, and everyone hurried home to their television sets. Even the fish and chip shops had "No Frying Tonight" signs on the doors, and the one espresso bar which she had passed was empty and unwelcoming.

Fortunately, her purse contained enough money to cover a night in a hotel. But having lost her bearings, she took some time to find her way back to the town centre. There was a hotel overlooking the market, and after making some attempt to tidy her bedraggled hair, she pushed through the revolving doors and approached the reception desk.

After the cold glistening streets, the atmosphere in the entrance lounge seemed overpoweringly close. Scent and cigar-smoke lingered in the air and mingled with odours from the grill-room.

"I'd like a single room, please," Joanna said briskly, to the clerk.

His experienced eyes took in her bedraggled appearance and the absence of luggage, then flickered to his watch.

"For how long, madam?" he enquired, without expression.

"I'm not sure yet. Probably only one night."

The clerk consulted a chart. "I'm very sorry, madam.

We haven't a single vacancy at present. Perhaps if you care to try one of the smaller commercial establishments . . ."

Joanna forced herself not to show her dismay. She felt sure the man was lying—he probably took her for a dubious character—but she wasn't going to argue.

"I see. Thank you," she said briefly, and turned away.

She was standing just outside the entrance, wondering if any of the smaller places were likely to view her with greater tolerance, when some men came out. They glanced at her without interest and continued their conversation. But the last one to emerge looked twice.

"Hello, Joanna. What are you doing here?" he exclaimed, in a friendly tone.

"Oh . . . hello, Dick. I—I'm just waiting for someone," she stammered.

Dick Drury glanced at his companions who were already halfway across the road, seemed about to excuse himself, then changed his mind.

"I say, are you all right?" he asked uncertainly. "You look a bit shaky."

"Do I? I don't feel it. I'm just a bit wet, that all," she answered hurriedly.

He peered at her more closely. "Wet! You're half drowned!" he exclaimed. "Who are you waiting for?"

"Well, I . . . that is . . ." Joanna fumbled for an adequate explanation but failed to find one.

"Look here, I'm not a fool. There's something wrong," Dick said bluntly. "No, don't start arguing. I'll get a taxi and we'll nip home to Margaret. You can explain what it's all about when you're out of that drenching raincoat and have a hot drink inside you."

And, as if he were afraid to leave her for fear she might run away, he bundled her back into the lounge and told the clerk to ring the cab rank.

Neither of them spoke during the short ride back to Connaught Street, and within ten minutes of finding her Dick was unlocking his front door and pushing Joanna ahead of him.

135

"Now take off your mac and your shoes and I'll get a dressing-gown," he ordered firmly.

The sounds of their arrival brought Margaret from the kitchen.

"You're early, darling," she began. Then, startled: "*Joanna!*"

"Get a dressing-gown and slippers, will you, Maggie— and some brandy, if there's any left," Dick said, without preamble.

He bent to switch on the fire, and after looking bewildered for a moment, Margaret disappeared to do his bidding.

"Please, Dick—I can't bother you," Joanna started distractedly.

"Don't be silly. We're your friends, aren't we?" he remarked cheerfully. "Now, come on, get out of that mac. You're flooding our valuable rug."

When Margaret came back and saw that the rain had penetrated to Joanna's dress, she insisted that it should come off too. So Dick went away to make coffee, and Joanna, too weary to protest any more, slipped out of her dress and peeled down her sopping nylons.

"Your feet are like ice. I'll give them a rub," Margaret said matter-of-factly. "What a night! It's more like January than August. Dick wasn't keen on going out, but he's Secretary of the Archaeological Society, you know, so he's more or less forced to turn up. I shouldn't think the meeting was very well attended tonight. Most of the members are on holiday this month. Still, I think it does him good to get away from the domestic atmosphere as much as possible"

She kept up a flow of light inconsequential chatter until Joanna began to look less pinched. Then, insisting that the younger girl should drink a sizeable shot of brandy, she went to find out how the coffee was progressing.

Neither of them attempted to question Joanna, and it was without any prompting on their part that she finally told them a version of the truth. Dick seemed very shocked by the news of Mrs. Carlyon's death, but Margaret, although she looked sad, expressed no surprise.

"Naturally, they're all very distressed and I'm sure they'd

rather be alone," Joanna concluded. "I know that technically I'm one of the family, but I still feel rather an interloper . . . so I left them." She stared into her coffee cup for some seconds, then said diffidently, "I haven't any right to ask it, but since I'm here, I wonder if you could possibly put me up. I—I can sleep on the couch, and it will only be for one night."

"Of course you can stay, my dear—but don't you think you ought to let them know where you are?" Margaret suggested gently. "You can't just walk out of the house without a word. They'll be worried stiff."

Joanna tensed. "No—no, they won't," she said tautly. "I—I told them——"

Margaret leaned forward and laid a hand on her arm. "Joanna, Charles has been here," she said quietly. "He came about nine o'clock. He'd already been on quite an extensive search for you, and he was at his wits' end."

The words were hardly out of her mouth before a car came scorching down the street and there was a squeal of brakes.

Joanna sprang up. "You've told him I'm here," she cried accusingly.

"Yes, Dick phoned from next door a few minutes ago," Margaret admitted. "We *had* to tell him, my dear."

Joanna moved swiftly towards the inner room, but was intercepted by Dick, who grabbed both her wrists. An instant later, the front door burst open and Charles appeared.

In the fraction of time before anyone spoke, Joanna knew exactly how it felt to be an animal at bay, or a criminal caught in his last refuge.

Then, quite quietly, Charles closed the door behind him. "Thank God you found her when you did," he said tersely to Dick.

"Charles, she's very tired and rather upset. Don't be——" Margaret began.

"I can guess how she's feeling," he cut in. "I'll take her back to my place. Mrs. Howard will look after her."

Dick was still holding Joanna's wrist, but only lightly now. She twisted free of him. "Do you mind *not* discussing me as if I'm an escaped lunatic?" she snapped furiously. She turned to Margaret. "You agreed to put me up for the night. Have you changed your mind about that?"

"Why, no, of course not—but if Charles thinks . . ."

"Charles has nothing to do with it," Joanna retorted harshly. "He isn't responsible for me." She fixed her eyes on the knot of Charles's tie. "I'm sorry if you've been anxious," she said coldly. "But you must have known that I'm perfectly capable of taking care of myself. There was certainly no need to start looking for me." Her voice shook slightly, and she cleared her throat. "If you will kindly arrange for my belongings to be sent to the station as early as possible tomorrow, I can pick them up when I catch the train for London."

There was another taut silence. Then, in a voice so quiet and even that it was far more unnerving than an angry roar, Charles said to Margaret, "Will you please tell Joanna that, in the circumstances, you can no longer accommodate her?"

Margaret's eyes widened. "But, Charles, if she doesn't want to . . ."

"Tell her, please, Margaret." His tone was still perfectly controlled and polite, but his eyes—as Joanna flashed a glance at him—had the glitter of total ruthlessness in them.

The Drurys exchanged a brief glance, and it was Dick who spoke.

"I'm sorry, Joanna, but if Charles thinks you'd be better at his place, we can't keep you here," he said slowly, looking very embarrassed.

"Dick, you can't mean that!" she exclaimed, aghast. "I—I thought you were *my* friends too. Why should you let him browbeat you?"

"We are your friends, Joanna," Margaret insisted. "But I'm sure Charles knows what's best for you."

There were tears of outrage and despair in Joanna's eyes, and she was almost choking on an uprush of impotent fury. But if she had been hanging from thumbscrews, she wouldn't have cried in front of Charles.

"Very well," she said quiveringly. "I'll go to a hotel."

"At this hour? In Margaret's dressing-gown?" Charles enquired mockingly.

"I think you must have been trying to get a room at the Grand, weren't you?" Dick said, more gently. "As Charles says, it's pretty late. You haven't a hope, my dear."

Suddenly Joanna knew that she couldn't go on fighting. The spurious flare of vitality engendered by the double brandy and coffee was flickering out, and she felt almost sick with fatigue.

"Oh, all right," she muttered hopelessly. "I'll go with him."

Five minutes later, after Margaret had insisted on wrapping her in a camel coat with a rug to cover her legs, she was driven away.

Charles spoke only once on the journey.

"When did you last eat?" he asked flatly.

"I—I can't remember. Oh, at lunch-time, I suppose," she answered uncaringly.

He did not comment.

By the time they reached his house, Joanna was afraid that she was actually going to *be* sick. There was a gnawing ache in her stomach and her head was swimming. So when Charles half lifted her out of the car, and then swung her up in his arms, she was too intent on fighting down her nausea to make even a token resistance.

Almost immediately after he had carried her inside, his housekeeper appeared from a back room. She followed them up the stairs and, dimly and without recognition, Joanna heard the little concerned clicking noises she was making with her tongue.

Then she was being lowered on to a blessedly soft bed and Charles was giving instruction about bread and milk and some aspirin.

What followed was only a blur. Somebody—not Charles—insisted that she tried the bread and milk, and fed her like a child. Then gradually the ache and the feeling of sickness went away, and she was helped into a nightdress. Finally, with her feet on a hot water bottle and her head on a pillow as soft as a cloud, she was tucked up. After that . . . sleep.

When Joanna woke up next morning, a plump little grey-haired woman, whom she seemed vaguely to recognise, was standing beside the bed.

"How do you feel this morning, Miss Allen?" she asked cheerfully.

"Oh . . . fine," Joanna replied, with some surprise. "I feel fine."

She struggled to sit up, and the woman gave her a helping hand and expertly plumped up the pillows.

"Perhaps I'd better introduce myself," she said, with a smile. "I'm Mrs. Howard, Mr. Carlyon's housekeeper."

"Oh, yes . . . the bread and milk," Joanna said, trying to recollect the events of the previous evening in greater detail. "What happened? Was I taken ill?"

"No, no. You were just very tired and rather overwrought. I don't think you'd had much to eat," Mrs. Howard said casually. "However, I've brought you a nice breakfast, so you won't feel like that today."

She handed Joanna a pretty turquoise silk bedjacket, helped her to slip it on, then placed a light wicker bed-table across her knees. On it, attractively set out on the immaculate linen tray cloth, was a glass of freshly-squeezed orange juice, a covered silver dish, a graceful Wedgwood coffee-pot and a matching cup and saucer. There was also a single yellow rosebud in a tiny crystal glass, and an untouched copy of a morning newspaper.

"If you want more toast or more coffee, just ring the bell," said the housekeeper, indicating a push-button by the head-board.

It was not until she had eaten every morsel of the deliciously buttery scrambled eggs which she had discovered in the warming-dish, and had spread a slice of the crisp yet not brittle toast, that Joanna took stock of her surroundings.

Last night, she had had a muddled impression of flowered chintz and a warm-coloured carpet. Now she saw that she was in a most delightful bedroom, so feminine and pretty that it could only have been planned by a woman, or a professional decorator.

The bed in which she was lying was a modern divan, but

140

it had four white-and-gold posts supporting a quilted silk canopy, and a matching coverlet was folded over an ottoman. The furniture was reproduction Louis Quinze with triple mirrors on the spindle-legged dressing-table, and there was an elegant chaise-longue upholstered in lemon velvet by the windows. Yes, definitely a woman's room in every detail from the Redouté flower prints and painted porcelain finger-plates to the fluffy white scatter-rugs and pleated voile lampshades.

Having examined the room, eaten some more toast—the butter was curled in dewy rolls, the marmalade vintage Oxford—Joanna inspected the bedjacket. It tied at the neck with hand-stitched silk rouleaux and the collar and cuffs were edged with narrow lace.

Underneath, she discovered, she was wearing a matching nightgown of double nylon, the under-layer splashed with white flowers, the over-layer sheer as gossamer.

Not the kind of garments which would normally be kept at hand for an unexpected and unprepared visitor—and certainly not in a bachelor household, she thought, puzzled.

She was drinking her second cup of coffee and trying to concentrate on the latest world news, when there was a light tap at the door and Charles walked in. Joanna jerked upright, almost dropped her cup and let the paper fall over the butter-dish.

"Good morning. Mrs. Howard tells me you're feeling much better," he remarked, coming to the bedside and pulling up a chair.

"Yes . . . yes, I am," Joanna said, flustered. She had not expected to have to face him till later—certainly not while she was still in bed, her hair uncombed and without a speck of make-up.

"Good. Do you mind if I smoke? I've only just finished breakfast myself."

"Not at all."

Charles lit a cigarette, reached for an oyster-shell ashtray and crossed his legs. Apparently he was not going to the factory today as it was already after ten and he was wearing a linen shirt, open at the neck, and whipcord slacks.

"As you doubtless realise, I want to have a talk with

you," he said presently. "However, if you don't yet feel up to it, you have only to say so."

Joanna remembered how relentlessly he had forced the Drurys' hand the night before. Pleasant as her surroundings might be, they were not of her own choice. She had been forced to come here, and so was under no real obligation to show gratitude.

Her tone was cool as she answered, "It depends on what you want to talk about."

"I should have thought that was obvious—what happened yesterday afternoon, of course."

She shifted slightly and he leaned forward and lifted the table from over her.

"Personally I think yesterday afternoon is better left alone," Joanna said flatly. "As I told you last night, I'm leaving Merefield—today. I think the best thing for all of us is to try to forget that I ever came here."

"Can *you* forget it?" he asked bluntly.

She fidgeted with the end of the sheet. "Perhaps not at once," she answered, in a low voice. "I don't expect you to believe it, but I grew very fond of . . . Mrs. Carlyon, in the short time I knew her."

"Why shouldn't I believe it? It was obvious. And she was very fond of you. Your coming here made all the difference to her," he said quietly.

Joanna stared at him. "But yesterday——"

"What happened yesterday was as horrifying to us as it was to you. You must know that, if you think about it. But when someone has been bottling up a grudge for more than twenty years, they aren't responsible for their actions when the repression finally snaps," he told her gravely. "Monica has been working up to this point since she and your mother were young girls. Her grief for her mother—which was perfectly genuine, of course—got all mixed up with her life-long resentment against Nina and the frustrations of her marriage. It was extremely unfortunate that you had to bear the brunt of the inevitable eruption, but it's probably just as well that it happened when it did. Now, after a spell in a good nursing home and a holiday well away from Merefield, she'll probably be much happier and more balanced than she's been since she was a child. If there hadn't been that scene and her subsequent collapse . . ." He concluded the sentence with an expressive gesture.

Joanna stared intently at the blanket. "But *you* looked so angry . . . as if you hated me," she said, at last.

Although it was only half smoked, Charles crushed out his cigarette with three short sharp jabs. "I don't hate you, Joanna," he said evenly. "I find you extremely exasperating at times, but I certainly don't hate you. If I looked angry, it was because I hated having to let you go through that ordeal. But it wouldn't have been wise to put a stop to it."

There was another silence.

"All the same I am leaving Merefield," Joanna told him. "I haven't mentioned it before, but I'm starting a season of cabaret at a hotel in London next month. I have to go down for rehearsals and fittings and so on."

"Was this arranged before you left Paris?"

"Yes, it was. To be frank, it was the chief reason why I agreed to come with you. My agent thought it would be a good idea for me to absorb some English atmosphere beforehand."

"I see," Charles said thoughtfully. But she couldn't tell whether the information displeased him or not. "But if Grandmother hadn't died, you wouldn't have left yet, would you?"

"Well, no—not quite so soon," she conceded.

"Then why change your plans?"

"Because I think it's the wisest course," she said flatly. "I—I don't want to go back to Mere House now."

"Then you can put up here," he said smoothly. "Mrs. Howard is a perfectly adequate chaperone."

"You *want* me to stay?" she asked, puzzled. A tiny flicker of hope was kindling inside her.

But it was swiftly dispelled by his reply. "Yes, I do. Frankly, I think Cathy should have someone with her— at least for the next few days. Grandmother was a very important person in her life, and she's at the age to take a sudden loss very hard. Vanessa will be spending most of her time at the nursing home—and she and Cathy have never been very close—so, unless you're around, the poor kid will have no one to distract her."

"I see," Joanna said dully. "But she'll have you. She . . . she adores you."

"I shall be pretty taken up with the arrangements for the funeral," he said tonelessly.

Suddenly Joanna realised that, in spite of his impassive manner, he too must be grieving for the old lady.

"Very well," she said swiftly. "I'll stay on a little longer."

"It might be a good idea if Cathy moved in here too," he suggested. "A change of surroundings is always a good idea in these circumstances."

"But what about Neal?" Joanna asked.

"He'll have to remain at Mere House. We can't leave Alice alone there. She has no family to go to, and it may take some time to find her another post."

"You're dismissing her?"

"No, of course not. But she doesn't want to stay now that Grandmother is dead, and the house is far too big for Monica's use—particularly when the children are all off her hands. I shall put it up for sale—probably as being suitable for offices—and find somewhere more compact for her." He paused and gave here a rather keen glance. "By the way, Neal will be leaving as soon as the funeral is over. He's decided that he can't stand the factory any longer and is going in for serious art."

Joanna drew in her breath. "Oh, Charles, that's wonderful," she exclaimed delightedly. "You mean you've agreed to finance him?"

"He'll have enough money to fix up a small studio and provide the bare necessities. But he certainly won't be in clover," Charles said drily.

"Oh, I'm so glad. I'm sure you won't regret it. He's shown me some of his work and, although I'm not an expert, I'm sure he has real talent."

"Maybe when you go to London you'll see something of him," Charles remarked.

"I doubt it. I'll be busy working and Neal will be painting furiously."

"Perhaps he ought to start by painting you. Once you've gone back to your career we're unlikely to see you again, I suppose, and if you become an international star, a portrait might be quite an asset," he said lightly. Then, getting up, "I must be off. I'll bring Cathy round for lunch, and pick up your belongings."

He was turning towards the door when Joanna called him back.

"Charles . . . I'm sorry I was so . . . so difficult last night. I didn't mean to make this time harder for you."

"That's all right," he said crisply. Then, his mouth curving slightly, "Oh, by the way, if you're wondering about this room and those night things—this is Maureen's bedroom, and the nightdress was to be her next birthday present."

"Maureen?" she asked blankly.

"My sister."

"I didn't know you had one."

He raised his eyebrows. "Haven't I mentioned her?"

"No one has."

"Oh, well, she's been off on her own for some time now and we tend to forget her for spells. Although she's a journalist, she's hopeless at writing letters." He glanced round the room, as if faintly amused by its extreme femininity. "However, she does descend on us occasionally, so we keep this room ready," he explained. "Actually this house is really hers. I'm only living here until I marry—if and when that happens."

"You mean if you marry you'll leave here?"

"Of course." He shrugged slightly. "Brides usually like to start a home from scratch, don't they? I've got some building land up on The Ridges, but whether I ever make use of it depends on . . . a lot of things."

And with that he left the room.

*   *   *

Two evenings later, Joanna and Cathy were sitting in

145

Charles's garden when Cathy said suddenly, "Joanna, is your career terribly important to you?"

It was such an unexpected question that Joanna couldn't answer for a moment. Until Cathy had broken their silence, she had been deep in some rather gloomy thoughts about life and the end of life.

Earlier in the day they had been among the large number of mourners at Mrs. Carlyon's funeral, for as well as being the widow of a former Mayor and important figure in the shoe industry, Mary Carlyon had been the kind of person who makes friends and admirers in every walk of life. Yet there had been nothing depressing about the simple burial service in the little country church about five miles outside Merefield. The sun had been shining and the birds singing as Mrs. Carlyon was laid to rest in the dappled shade of an ancient sycamore. As the rector of the parish had told them, she had been a kind and honourable woman who had lived a full life and was now deservedly at peace.

"I don't know, Cathy," Joanna said slowly, rousing herself from her unwonted introspection. " 'Important' is such a relative word to apply to anything. I enjoy my job and I want to be as successful as possible. If one isn't moderately keen, there isn't much point in doing something."

"I mean would you be terribly unhappy if you had to stop it?" Cathy qualified. "Would it be the . . . the end of the world for you?"

"No, hardly that," Joanna said, smiling a little. "I should feel rather lost, I expect, but nothing is ever 'the end of the world,' as you put it! Anyway, why this catechism?"

"Oh . . . I just wondered," Cathy said vaguely. "I've been thinking about *my* career, actually. I want to be an actress more than anything—only they never seem to be very lucky in their private lives, do they?"

She paused for some moments, plucking at some blades of grass below her deck chair. "It must be so nice to have a husband and children and all be happy together. Some of the girls at school have homes like that, and—well, you can sort of *feel* it when you go to tea with them."

Joanna felt a sudden rush of compassion for her. Poor little Cathy! She hadn't put it into words, but she obviously

146

envied the friends whose families were more united than her own. Joanna knew just how she felt. She too had ached for the intangible warmth and security of a loving family circle when she was that age.

"Oh, I'm quite sure lots of actresses have very happy private lives," she said cheerfully. "It's just that, for some peculiar reason, the miserable ones are better news value!"

Cathy leaned back in her chair and gazed up at the sky. "I wonder what it's like to be madly in love?" she murmured. "Have you ever been in love, Joanna?"

"'In love' is as relative as 'important'," Charles said suddenly, from close behind them.

He must have been standing there since the conversation started, Joanna realised.

"Well, have you, Joanna?" he persisted, coming round to the front of them and dropping into the third chair that had been put out.

But Cathy saved her from answering. "I bet lots of people have been in love with *you*," she announced decidedly. Then, with a deep sigh, "I wish I had red hair and nice legs."

Joanna laughed. "What's wrong with your legs, may I ask?"

"They're so bony—my knees are like rocks. And my hair is like chewed string."

"No, it isn't, silly," Joanna countered. "It's rather a lovely honey colour. Besides, later on, if you really want to change it, you can try a red rinse, or even a black one. If one's born with red hair one can't have any variety."

Mrs. Howard came out with a tray of cold drinks and some sandwiches. Nobody had had much appetite for lunch and there was an hour to go before supper.

"Oh, that reminds me, I have something for you," Charles said to Joanna. "Alice was checking the drawers in your room at Mere House and she found these tucked away at the back of one of them. Hadn't you missed them?"

He handed her the shagreen box containing Yves's parting gift.

Joanna flushed. "Thanks. No, I hadn't," she said shortly.

147

"What is it? Jewellery? Can I see?" Cathy asked inquisitively.

Joanna hesitated for a moment, then passed her the box.

"Gosh! How super! They aren't . . . they can't be real sapphires," Cathy exclaimed.

"Why shouldn't they be real?" Charles asked negligently, his eyes resting on Joanna with a faintly malicious expression.

"Well, I didn't think you earned as much as that," Cathy explained to Joanna. A thought occurred to her. "Perhaps they were a present from one of your fans, were they? An infatuated French millionaire, like that man who sent two dozen deep red roses every day to some actress. There was a piece about it in a magazine. He died in the end—the millionaire, I mean—but he put a thingummy in his will and, instead of roses, she now gets two dozen white orchids. Gosh, he must have been terribly in love with her." She examined the ear-rings again. "I say, I suppose I couldn't possibly try them on, could I—just for a second?"

"Yes, if you like," Joanna said, forced to smile at the hesitant tone of the request. She fished a mirror out of her bag so that Cathy could inspect the effect.

"Oh, they look quite ordinary on me," the younger girl said disappointedly. "I just haven't got the face for sapphires. You put them on, Joanna. I can't think why you didn't wear them at our party."

"No, I don't think I will just now," Joanna said, carefully casual. "Sparkling jewellery never does look very good in daylight—and these don't really suit me."

For some reason she could not analyse, she could not bring herself to wear the ear-rings in front of Charles.

*   *   *

It was about nine o'clock and Charles had just advised Cathy to have an early night, when the younger girl suddenly said, "I wish you hadn't got to go to London, Joanna. Couldn't you possibly tell them you don't want to work at this hotel place, and stay here with us?"

Joanna turned away from the window where she had been watching a pair of swallows skimming in search of insects.

148

"I wish I hadn't got to go, too," she said gently. "But I have a contract, you see, and how could I earn my living if I stayed in Merefield?"

Cathy scratched a midge bite on one thin brown arm. She seemed about to say something, then changed her mind. Finally, she said, "No, I suppose you couldn't. Oh, well—goodnight."

After she had gone, there was a long silence. Charles seemed deep in a book, and Joanna returned to the window. Recently—with the exception of that brief exchange in the garden earlier on—there had been no clashes between them. But she doubted if the truce had much significance. They were still living under the shadow of her grandmother's death, and were not in the mood for fireworks.

"Did you mean that—about wishing you could stay here?" Charles asked suddenly.

Joanna turned. He had thrust his book aside and was reaching for a cigarette. He looked tired and rather strained, she thought. Suddenly, a snatch of conversation which she had had with Cathy soon after her arrival came back into her mind. What was it Cathy had said? Something about Charles being the person they all had to kow-tow to.

At the time, Joanna remembered, the remark had confirmed her opinion that Charles was something of a despot.

Now she saw that, even if he was a shade despotic, his way was generally the right one. And where would they all have been after her grandmother's death without Charles to take charge and make plans?

"Perhaps it's because I've never lived in a place like Merefield before," she said slowly, evading a direct answer to his question. "It's so much more peaceful than a big city, don't you think? One doesn't—isn't bound to rush about, to . . . to compete with everybody." She smiled and her tone was airy. "Maybe, at heart, I'm a small town girl —or maybe it's just a novelty."

Charles watched the smoke rising from the tip of his cigarette. "If you'd really like to stay, it isn't impossible."

It was like the other morning when he had come to her bedroom and asked her to postpone her departure. Her pulses began to race and she had difficulty in breathing evenly.

"What do you mean?"

The interval between her question and his reply could only have been a few seconds, but it seemed an eternity of tension.

"I happen to know that Grandmother has left you some money. Not a fortune, but enough to maintain you for a year or two."

"I see." It took all her control not to burst into wild peals of half-hysterical laughter. You fool, Joanna Allen! she thought bitterly. That's the second time you've let yourself in for an unwitting rebuff. What did you expect? That he was going to fall on his knees and implore you to marry him?

It was a moment or two before she could be certain that her voice wouldn't crack. Then she said coolly, "That was very kind of Grandmother. I had no idea. But somehow I can't see myself leading a life of leisure, and I'm still really more French than English, you know. I wouldn't want to settle here and then find myself desperately nostalgic for Paris. And now, if you don't mind, I'll go up to bed, too. Goodnight, Charles."

Without waiting for his answer, she went swiftly out of the room.

*　　　*　　　*

The following afternoon, Mrs. Howard summoned her to the telephone. The call was from Gustave Hugo. He wanted her to meet him in London in forty-eight hours.

When Cathy heard the news, she was disconsolate. But Charles accepted it with his customary calm.

"You must let us know when you are due to appear on television. We shall want to watch you," he said casually.

To Joanna that last day and night in Merefield were the most subtle emotional torture she had ever experienced. If this was loving someone, she would never be caught a second time. And at their final breakfast together she felt like a condemned prisoner with the minutes ticking her life away.

150

At the last moment Cathy said abruptly that she didn't want to come to the station after all. She looked on the verge of tears.

"Oh, Joanna, shall we ever see you again?" she asked forlornly, as Charles carried the bags out to the car.

"Why, yes, I expect so, dear. Maybe . . . maybe when you're older you could come on a visit to Paris."

"We'd better be off. We haven't too much of a margin," Charles warned, coming back into the hall.

Joanna gave Cathy a brief hug. "Don't forget to write and tell me what you think of the TV show," she said unsteadily.

Then they were in the car and driving swiftly to the station.

Mercifully, Charles didn't prolong their goodbyes. He found the seat she had reserved, swung her bags on the rack and stepped out of the compartment again.

"I won't hang about, Joanna," he said briskly, shutting the door. "Good luck with your new show, and . . . thanks for coming."

"Goodbye, Charles." She bent to the window and held out her hand.

His lean fingers closed strongly but briefly over hers.

"Goodbye."

Joanna hung out of the window and watched him return to the barrier, but he never looked back. At last, when his tall broad-shouldered figure was lost to sight, she slumped into her seat and closed her eyes.

She was still sitting limply in her corner when the collector came in to check her ticket. There was one thing which was "the end of the world," she had discovered. That was leaving the man you loved because he didn't love you, and most likely never seeing him again.

*   *   *

On the first of September, a few days before her opening night, Joanna walked down Piccadilly to buy gloves at Fortnum and Mason. She had expected London to compare unfavourably with Paris. But although, architecturally, it was not as beautifully laid out as the fabled City of Light, it

151

had a character all of its own which she found most delightful.

Whoever had started the legend that Englishmen were uncouth? she wondered, admiring the many immaculately-tailored, bowler-hatted business men who passed her in the streets. And why was the bowler hat such a joke abroad? It seemed to her most becoming.

But thinking about Englishmen, even in the mass, was dangerous ground. It was better to contemplate the women and girls, and they were certainly quite as chic as their Parisian counterparts.

France might have the greatest fashion houses, but if you couldn't afford *haute couture*, you had to rely on the skill of some "little woman"; and "little women" were not always as marvellous as they were said to be. Here, in London, the windows of the big stores were full of extremely well-made "off the peg" garments at, so it seemed to Joanna, incredibly cheap prices.

She spent most of her free time searching out blissful tweed skirts and lambswool sweaters, or browsing in antique shops or just seeing all the sights. She was always busy: always going somewhere or doing something. But she was still utterly wretched.

On this particular afternoon, she bought her gloves and then lingered on the ground floor grocery department—if one could apply such a humdrum term to the pink marble and soft carpets, the frock-coated assistants and mink-wrapped customers of that gourmets' Mecca. After wandering round the cold buffet section where one could order almost anything from a full-scale banquet to a very special picnic hamper, she went out into the sun and strolled leisurely up to the Ritz.

Gustave, who seemed to know London as well as he did Paris, complained that even the best hotels and restaurants were becoming grossly overcrowded. But the Ritz was the last bastion of a more gracious era. There one could find proper elbow room, and did not have to shout one's conversation over a hubbub of other voices.

Joanna went in by the Piccadilly entrance and, being five minutes early, decided to freshen her make-up. Like Fortnum and Mason's *épicerie,* the cloakroom seemed to have been hewn out of a huge block of rosy marble. Leaving her parcels in the care of the attendant, she sat down at a large gilded looking-glass and examined her reflection.

Fortunately Gustave didn't seem to have noticed it, but she was far from looking her best. She had lost a good deal of weight, and it took an elaborate make-up to disguise the hollowing of her cheeks and the dullness of her eyes.

I can't go on like this, she thought worriedly. I shall have to get a prescription for some sleeping pills.

"You have taken up smoking, I see?" Gustave remarked, when they had finished their tea.

"You don't object, do you?" Joanna asked warily, fitting her cigarette into a short amber holder.

"It is not a habit I admire in women," he said bluntly. "But at least you are not one of these." He gave a brief imitation of a woman with a cigarette dangling from a corner of her mouth and one eye screwed up against smoke. "Ah, believe me, such manners are quite common—even here. See, at that table." He indicated a pair of middle-aged women of extreme elegance who were seated close by; one of them was smoking exactly as he had demonstrated.

"Tell me, *chérie*, when did it become necessary for you to smoke?" he asked.

Joanna stiffened. "It isn't necessary exactly," she said airily. "But most people do nowadays and . . . and I find it relaxing."

"Hmph!" He gave her a shrewd glance, but didn't pursue the point.

It was not until they were on the point of leaving and Joanna was drawing on her gloves that he said abruptly, "Enough of these evasions. We both know that matters are not right—and we both know the reason. The time has arrived to discuss it."

"The reason?" Joanna said, mystified.

There was a gleam of sardonic amusement in Gustave's eyes. "One does not become so noticeably debilitated *without* a reason," he said drily. "No, please don't try to insist that you are filled with radiance. Permit me to tell

153

you, *ma petite,* that not only do you look like an owl—those circles under the eyes are not *à la mode* at present—but also you begin to sing like one."

Joanna sighed. She might have known that Gustave would detect that she was off form.

"I'm sorry," she began wearily. "Perhaps I'm a bit run down. I'd better——"

Gustave held up his hand. "I have noted the symptoms, I have diagnosed the condition—and I am about to effect a cure," he announced. "Immediately after your first appearance, you will retire to your suite. You will, I am confident, have had an enthusiastic reception. And for success, there must be some rewards. Yours, *ma chère Janine,* will include a delectable supper, some very good champagne—and an ecstatic reunion with your handsome young de Mansard!"

Joanna was horror-struck. *"Yves!"* she exclaimed. "Oh, Gustave, what have you been up to?"

But for once the agent was too delighted with his own deep-laid schemes to notice her consternation.

"You had no sooner left Paris," he explained, "than I was besieged—but positively besieged—by this most ardent young man. Having discovered that you were not in Brittany, he insisted on knowing where you were. When I refused to tell him, he was extremely angry—he even became quite violent. However, assuming that you had parted on bad terms and that you, at least, were not anxious to repair the breach, I remained adamant. But when I come to London—ah, now the situation has changed. Janine is pale and listless. Janine is busy all day, but does not seem to sleep. She smokes. She fidgets. She is clearly very unhappy. It is evident that Monsieur de Mansard is not alone in his desire for a reconciliation."

"But, Gustave——"

"So I have arranged it," he continued, ignoring her interruption. "And when a woman sings to the man she loves, she cannot fail to be ravishing," he ended happily.

Feeling as if all the breath had been knocked out of her, Joanna leaned her elbows on the table and buried her face in her hands.

Gustave seemed to think she was overcome by delighted

emotion as he patted her shoulder and said kindly, "Do not weep, *ma mie*. You have shed enough tears already. Now it is time for the happy ending."

She straightened. "I'm not weeping, Gustave. I'm just . . . completely bowled over."

And then, on the point of telling him that he had made a ghastly error of judgment that would not help her and would probably agonise Yves, she held back.

All Gustave really cared about was her success as an artist. He would go—and had already gone—to extraordinary lengths to ensure that success. Indeed, if she told him the truth, even without mentioning Charles by name, he was more than capable of rushing off to Merefield and tracking him down. If she wasn't in love with Yves, he would reason, then it must be someone in England.

The only thing to do was to counterfeit as much delight as she could muster, and try to brace herself up.

"Come, I'll take you back to the hotel where you can rest," Gustave said briskly. "And dream of the many tender exchanges which will take place at the end of the week," he added, chuckling.

* * *

An hour before her début, Joanna sat in her room in the hotel feeling strangely calm. Gustave had just left her after a final pep-talk. And although she didn't think she had made a very good job of exuding delighted anticipation since his bombshell about Yves, the agent seemed bursting with confidence.

Yves would have arrived in London by now, she supposed. When she made her entrance, he and Gustave would be sharing a table. Oh, lord! What would it do to him when she had to explain that it was all a mistake, and she had not changed her mind. It was probably her dread of the reunion with him that had pushed out all first-night nerves.

Presently she took a tepid bath and began to make up her face. The spectacular gown which Gustave had ordered for her was hanging in a muslin shroud in the wardrobe. It was made of deep primrose lace, heavily embroidered with tiny gold beads and crystal *paillettes* and pearls, and after clinging from bosom to knee, it suddenly burst out

155

into a froth of spangled net flounces which formed a sweeping fish-tail. With it, she was to wear long white kid gloves and high-heeled gold slippers. Her hair, which she had insisted on dressing herself, would be piled high and speared with fragile pearl butterflies.

There was half an hour to go and Joanna was adding an extra flick of eye-liner to her lids, when there was a soft scratch at the outer door.

She slipped her kimono over her wispy undergarments. "Who is it, please?" she called from the door to her bedroom.

There was no answer, but after a brief interval the door was cautiously opened.

"Hello. Can I come in?" Cathy asked shyly.

"Cathy—darling! What in the world are you doing here?" Without waiting for a reply, Joanna enveloped her in a delighted embrace. Then, standing back a little, she said, "You're the *last* person I expected to see. What a lovely surprise."

"I'm not supposed to be up here," Cathy admitted, with an anxious glance over her shoulder. "They said downstairs that you couldn't see anyone—not anyone. But I thought you wouldn't mind me, so I slipped up secretly. I say, you do look different with all that make-up on."

"I'm very glad you did slip up. I'm beginning to get the jitters," Joanna said, making a face. "But don't you want to see the show? I'll see if I can fix it." She moved towards the telephone.

"Oh, that's all arranged," Cathy told her. "We didn't think we'd be able to get a table, but a friend of Maureen's —he's a journalist too—used his influence to get us in."

Joanna's heart seemed to plunge. "Us?" she repeated. "Who else is with you? Neal?"

CHAPTER SEVEN

"NO, Neal's still at home. He was all set to come to London and start painting when he suddenly burst out in spots." Cathy giggled. "Isn't it a scream? He's got measles." Then she frowned. "I say, I hope you've had them, Joanna. I have, but I might be a carrier."

"I don't know, I expect so." Joanna didn't care. She was quivering with suppressed impatience, and could have shaken Cathy for her obtuseness.

The younger girl was glancing round the sitting-room. "Wow! What a swanky place this is—and a *gold* telephone!" she exclaimed, greatly impressed. Then, catching sight of the clock, "Gosh, I must fly. I'm supposed to be spending a penny, but I've been away ages. Well, lots of luck, Joanna. I'm sure you'll be terrific."

"Cathy—wait!" Joanna cried sharply. "You still haven't told me who brought you."

"Charles, of course. Who else?" Cathy peered out of the door to see if the coast was clear. "Can we come up and see you afterwards, or will you be too tired?"

"Of course not. Come up straight away and we'll have a party."

"Ooh—lovely! Well . . . 'bye for now."

Joanna watched Cathy run furtively along the corridor and duck down a staircase. Then she closed the outer door and walked dazedly back to the bedroom.

He was here! She was going to see him again! *Oh, Charles—darling Charles!—if you knew how I'd missed you,* she thought dreamily.

The telephone rang. "Ten minutes to go, Miss Alain." It was the voice of the cabaret manager.

"Thank you. I'm almost ready." Joanna replaced the receiver, and moved swiftly to the wardrobe.

157

She pressed the floor-service bell, and by the time she had put on her dress a maid had arrived to zip her up.

"Thanks. Is my back view all right?" she asked, beginning to feel butterflies fluttering inside her.

The woman inspected her. "Yes, miss, you look lovely. Oh, thank you very much, miss—" as Joanna pressed a generous tip into her hand—"and good luck for your opening."

The telephone rang again. "Five minutes, Miss Alain."

"I'm just coming down." Joanna used a professional gloss on her lips, smoothed an eyebrow and sprayed on a final touch of scent.

Then, standing back from the mirror, she took a last critical glance at herself. The dress was perfect. She looked like a sophisticated mermaid, and the primrose lace with its shimmering embroidery was the perfect foil for her vivid hair and smooth honey-gold skin. Now—since Cathy's surprise appearance—it wasn't only the special corneal drops that made her eyes sparkle, or rouge that warmed her cheeks.

Two minutes later she stepped out of the service lift to find the cabaret manager waiting for her. He didn't have to tell her that she looked beautiful. Accustomed as he was to theatrical glamour, he was still capable of responding to that extra something—the indefinable but infinitely compelling "star" quality which Gustave had been the first to discern.

The artists made their entrance by way of curving stairs which led down on to the dance floor. The idea had been copied from the famous staircase at the fabulous Café de Paris, and Joanna knew that the first descent to the floor was something of an ordeal—even for a recognised "name."

But, as she stood behind the curtains at the top, and listened to the clash of cymbals and the announcement, all nervousness evaporated. If Gustave could have read her thoughts at that moment, he would probably have been horrified. Because, suddenly, it didn't matter whether she was a success or not. Her whole future career might hang on the next twenty minutes—but that was totally unimportant. All she wanted—all she would ever want—was to stir the heart of one man.

" . . . so here she is, ladies and gentlemen. Mademoiselle Janine Alain!"

The curtains were swept aside, the orchestra burst into a special arrangement of *J'attendrai* and a single amber spotlight swept up the gilded staircase and focused on the slender glittering figure at the top. Joanna was "on."

Afterwards, she could remember very little about the first part of her performance. It had been rehearsed so intensively that every movement and gesture and glance came as automatically as breathing. And, as soon as her eyes had adjusted to the brilliant light, she began searching the tables—each lit by a dim rose-shaded lamp—for the one at which Charles and Cathy sat.

It was in the break before her last number that she saw them, seated near the back of the restaurant in one of the alcoves. Then, as the applause for her previous number died down, she moved to the foot of the staircase, mounted three steps and swept the train of her dress into a graceful drape.

"Thank you," she said quietly. "And now, a new song —which, like all the best songs, is about—love."

Gustave had been dubious about including this particular number in her repertoire. In sharp contrast to her earlier songs, which had all been gay and amusing and provocative, this one was purely romantic and, in his opinion, too unsophisticated for the type of audience she would be entertaining. But it had a lovely haunting tune and was the only song which gave full expression to the range of her voice, so she had managed to overcome his doubts.

Now, leaning lightly against the curving balustrade, she began the plaintive introduction.

"So many parties, so many dates,

Each night a new rendezvous.

Then came the evening I'll always remember

When I turned my head and saw—you!

The man I had searched for, the man in a million,

The man of my dreams—come true!"

Slowly, while the orchestra led into the lilting melody, Joanna turned and moved up another two stairs. Then, looking straight towards Charles, forgetting all the stylised methods of "putting over" a number, and standing completely still with her hands clasped at her breast, she sang the first two verses.

"Until we met, I didn't know

That you would set my heart aglow

Like this.

It can't be just the moonlight, it must be love—at last!

You touched my hand, I touched a star,

Now happiness is where you are,

Unless

It's only I who feels my heart—take wings!"

The strings swept into a reprise, and the spotlight followed her up to the top of the stairs. If there was any restiveness among the audience, she was not aware of it. Her whole being was intent on giving the words their full meaning, on making her voice the instrument to express her own helpless love.

"Until we kiss, how can I tell

If love has also cast its spell

On you?

Oh, if you feel it, say you feel it—soon!"

The last appealing note rose high and pure. Then Joanna's hands slipped down to her sides, and she inclined her head. For perhaps five seconds there was a kind of breathless hush—then resounding applause. Applause that seemed to go on and on, like waves breaking on a beach. Joanna bowed and smiled, and bowed again to the orchestra. But when the sustained clapping finally began to subside and the leader raised his baton in an interrogative gesture, she shook her head, bowed for the last time and slipped swiftly between the curtains.

Behind the scenes, the dapper little cabaret manager was exuding delight from every pore.

"Marvellous . . . marvellous!" he exclaimed, seizing her hands and pumping them delightedly. "They not only liked you, Miss Alain—they were entranced. And there are several very influential people here tonight, you know. The word will get round in no time. We shall be booked out every night."

"Thank you. I certainly hope so," Joanna said shakily. "And now, if you don't mind, I'd like to go up to my room. I—I've been rather keyed up."

"Naturally . . . naturally." He ushered her back to the lift, still beaming with satisfaction. "However, if I may make a suggestion, I'd be inclined to have a reasonably early call tomorrow morning. There are bound to be several requests for interviews—we may need to arrange a Press conference. It isn't every night that a star is born, you know."

As the lift door closed on his gleeful face, Joanna drew in a deep breath. Tomorrow seemed a century away. The climax of today was still to come.

In her room, she hurried to the dressing-table and quickly blotted away the sheen of moisture on her temples and upper lip. There wasn't time to change her make-up. She could only hold her wrists under the cold tap for a few moments, and then rub a stick of frozen cologne round the base of her throat.

A tap at the door brought her running through from the bedroom. But it was only a waiter wheeling a small trolley. On it, with a card expressing the compliments of the management, was a magnum bottle of champagne in a bucket of ice, and an elaborate arrangement of golden roses.

She had to wait another five nerve-racking minutes before there was another knock.

"Oh, Joanna you were *wonderful!*" Cathy exclaimed, flinging her arms round her.

Joanna laughed and returned the enthusiastic hug. But her eyes were looking over Cathy's head. Tall and incredibly distinguished-looking in the severe black and white of his evening kit, Charles was standing on the threshold. And the way he was looking at her made Joanna's heart leap like a mad thing.

"Crikey! Champagne!" As Cathy drew away, her eyes fell on the trolley. "And what gorgeous flowers." She darted forward to examine them.

161

Joanna held out her hand. "Hello, Charles," she said breathlessly. "Did you enjoy the show?"

He took both her hands, and his eyes were brilliant and intent.

"What can I say?" he asked softly. "You were superb, Joanna."

Her hands trembled in his, and her pulses raced. *For you,* she thought—*because you were there, my darling.*

She could have stood there for ever, just looking at him. But with Cathy present, she could only smile and say, "Thank you."

"I've never had champagne," Cathy informed her.

"Well, if Charles will open the bottle, we'll all have some," Joanna said gaily. "The glasses are in this cupboard."

"Don't forget to keep the cork," Cathy said earnestly, as Charles filled three glasses. "They're supposed to be lucky, aren't they?"

"Of course I shall keep it. It's not every day that people come hundreds of miles to see me. This is an occasion."

"Were you glad we were here, or did it put you off—being watched by relations?" Cathy asked.

Charles handed Joanna one of the glasses, and she looked straight into his eyes. "No, it didn't put me off. It gave me courage. Now, what shall we drink to?"

"To you, of course," Cathy said conclusively. She glanced expectantly at Charles.

He raised his glass and his smile was like a caress. "To you, Joanna Allen," he said quietly.

"To you," Cathy echoed, and they both drank.

It was then that there was a third knock on the door and Gustave's voice could be heard from outside in the corridor. Joanna closed her eyes. In the crazy exalted mood which had caught and absorbed her for the past hour, she had completely forgotten that Gustave would also be coming up to congratulate her, and with him Yves de Mansard.

For one mad moment, she was tempted to lock the door and call through that she couldn't be disturbed. But she

162

knew it was impossible. There was nothing to do but admit the two other men and pray—pray!—for the millionth chance that Charles wouldn't recognise the Frenchman. Or that if her did, it wouldn't take away the look that had been in his eyes a moment ago.

"Janine . . . ah, Janine, you were magnificent!" As soon as he opened the door, Gustave was embracing and congratulating her. "It is exactly as I thought," he exclaimed buoyantly. "Tonight you had magic! Tonight you became a star! Now there is no limit to our successes!"

He was so overwrought with enthusiasm that it was several minutes before he had calmed sufficiently to notice Charles and Cathy. Joanna introduced them. Then she turned to Yves.

"Hello, Yves. I didn't know you were in London. How are you?" she said evenly.

He bowed and kissed her fingertips. "You were enchanting, Janine," he said gravely.

"So you, I take it, are the Englishman who found Janine in Paris and restored her to her family?" Gustave said cordially to Charles.

"That's right." Charles's tone was clipped. He was looking at Yves, Joanna saw, and it was agonisingly clear that he had recognised him instantly.

Yves, too, was finding something familiar about the tall Englishman.

"But, Janine, isn't this the gentleman who called at your dressing-room on your last night at the Cordiale?" he enquired, in some perplexity. "Why didn't you tell me that he was a kinsman?" He turned to Charles, his expression amused. "It seems I owe you an apology, *m'sieur*. As I recollect, I almost threw you out."

"I believe you considered it," Charles agreed, with a not of derision in his tone.

The innuendo was clear, and Yves flushed. He turned to Cathy. "And you, *mademoiselle*?" he enquired, covering his hostility to Charles with a charming smile at the younger girl. "You are also one of Janine's mysterious English relatives?"

His smiling blue eyes and engaging French accent were

163

too much for Cathy's composure. Blushing to the lobes of her ears, she stammered confirmation.

"B-but her real name is Joanna, you know," she corrected breathlessly.

"Is that so?" Yves raised an eyebrow, and returned his attention to Joanna. "But I think Janine suits you better," he said. "Joe is for a boy, is it not? And Anna is one of these cold unfeminine names that the Germans give their women. Janine is all French—and you are French at heart . . . yes?"

Before Joanna could reply, Charles said briskly, "It's time you were in bed, Cathy."

"Oh, but Charles——"

"It's gone midnight and you've been up since seven o'clock." There was a note of steel in his voice.

"Yes, it is late and Janine, too, must be fatigued," Gustave agreed. "I also must leave." He clapped Yves on the shoulder. "Do not keep her up too late, *mon ami*. To-morrow will be another busy day." He kissed his fingers to Joanna. "You have exceeded all my hopes, *ma mie*. I am a very happy man. Goodnight."

"Goodnight, Gustave." Joanna turned to Charles and Cathy. "You—you aren't going straight back to Merefield, are you?" she asked, in a strained voice, speaking to them both and looking at a point somewhere between them. She couldn't bear to see that cold indifference on Charles's face again.

"Not immediately. I have some business matters to deal with before we go home," he said crisply. "Say goodnight, Cathy."

The younger girl seemed to have grasped that somehow the evening had gone sour. She gave Joanna a wan smile, muttered her goodnight and let Charles steer her out of the door.

He gave Joanna a final expressionless glance. "Goodnight . . . *Janine*," he said negligently.

And then they were gone, and she was alone with Yves.

* * *

"May I help myself to some of your champagne?" the

Frenchman enquired, after the door had closed and Joanna had stood staring at it in silence for some moments.

"Oh . . . yes, do," she answered heavily. Then, brushing a hand wearily over her forehead, "It's been quite an evening. Do you mind if I get out of this thing?"—with a distasteful downward glance at her primrose lace dress.

"By all means. Are you hungry? Shall I order some food while you are changing?"

At that moment, Joanna felt that she would never be hungry again. But she said flatly, "Yes, a good idea," and went into the bedroom.

But for Yves's presence, she would have flung herself on the bed and burst into tears of desolation. She felt rather like a rocket that has been spinning up to the stars and then abruptly fizzled out.

When she returned to the sitting-room, her face bare of make-up and the shabby cotton kimono belted over pyjamas, Yves was standing out on the tiny balcony. A second trolley bearing cold chicken sandwiches, a bowl of salad and a coffee-pot was ranged alongside the first.

Lighting a cigarette, Joanna stepped on to the balcony and leaned her elbows on the balustrade. Except for an occasional taxi going past, the street below was quiet. The lights in the windows of the shops on the opposite pavement had long been extinguished, and a policeman was pacing on his beat, pausing at every doorway to make sure the locks were secure.

"Janine, what did Gustave tell you about my coming here?" Yves asked suddenly.

Joanna straightened. At first, deep in her own misery, she had not been sensitive to his state of mind. But now she had a feeling that something was not quite as it should be—or as she would have anticipated. If she had considered the situation before it had come about, she would have expected Yves to attempt to embrace her as soon as the door closed on the others. But he had made no effort to touch her. And now, as they stood side by side on the narrow starlit balcony, he seemed uneasy—perhaps even nervous.

She turned back into the sitting-room. "He told me that when you found I wasn't in Brittany, you insisted on knowing where I had gone. He said he refused to tell you until he decided to ask you to come over for tonight."

"I see," Yves said slowly. "Yes, it is true that when I first discovered you were not in Brittany I was very disturbed and anxious. I still hoped that your answer to my . . . proposal was not final, you see."

Joanna wondered if there was such a thing as feminine intuition, or if her present instinct was based on wishful thinking. She took a chance.

"But now you have accepted that it was?" she said cautiously.

He gave her a startled glance. "No . . . no, not at all. If you have changed your mind——" He ended the sentence with a gesture. But he had flushed again, and she saw him swallow as if bracing himself.

"Gustave shouldn't have interfered. He jumped to some wrong conclusions and acted before I could correct them," she said awkwardly. "I'm sorry, Yves—I haven't changed my mind."

"You haven't?" he repeated swiftly.

She had a distinct impression that there was a note of relief in his voice.

"But I'm beginning to think that you have changed yours," she said reflectively.

It was probably a good fifteen years since Yves had blushed. But he did so now, and looked—incongruously—like a sheepish schoolboy caught out in some shameful escapade.

Then, seeing that Joanna was still quite calm and amiable, he drew a breath and admitted, "Well, to be frank with you, *chérie,* it is not so much that *I* have changed my mind, but that . . . that my circumstances have altered."

Joanna poured two cups of coffee and sat down on the sofa. "Let's clear up the whole situation, shall we?" she suggested. "What circumstances?"

Yves tasted the coffee and grimaced. "The fact is, Janine, that I have got myself engaged," he explained uncomfortably.

"Engaged!" Joanna gaped at him. "Well . . . that was quick work," she said drily.

"Please . . . it is not as you imagine. I was entirely serious when I asked you to marry me, and believe me, if I had thought there was a chance of your relenting I would never have taken this step." He gave a rather forlorn smile. "But since I know you very well, I did not have much hope that you would change. Oh, yes, I demanded that Hugo should tell me where you were. But that was only for a few days. By the end of the week, when you had not written or telephoned, I had begun to resign myself."

"And by the end of a fortnight you had discovered a more likely prospect," Joanna remarked, with a quizzical look.

"No, as it happens I have known Marie-Blanche all my life," he answered seriously. "She is considerably younger than I—not yet nineteen—and until recently I had regarded her as a child. However, at about the same time you left Paris, she came back from her finishing school in Switzerland. When I met her again, I realised that she was grown-up."

He paused, smiling faintly, as if at the recollection of something both funny and tender.

"I should explain that it has long been the wish of our parents that we should marry," he went on. "There would be mutual benefits, you understand. Naturally I thought the idea absurd, and nowadays even the more strictly-bred French girls are beginning to rebel against these *mariages de convenance*. But it seems that she has accepted the prospect of marrying me since she was quite small. I must say I do not approve of them putting such ideas into her head," he added, with a note of censure.

"You mean she's in love with you," Joanna put in gently.

He shrugged. "How can a chit of that age be in love with a man she scarcely knows? he countered impatiently. "It is a form of hero-worship, I suppose, although God knows she has chosen a poor hero. I only hope I may not disillusion her too badly."

"I don't think you'll disillusion her at all, Yves." Joanna reached out and patted his hand. "If you weren't such a nice person at heart, I wouldn't have liked you so well. I have an idea that your little Marie-Blanche may be the very person to bring out your best qualities. What is she like, and when is the wedding?"

He turned his head to look at her, and although he smiled, there was something in his eyes that told her he was still more than half hers. As yet it was only the formality of the betrothal and a blend of tenderness and protectiveness that bound him to his youthful fiancée. But, given time . . .

"She is not at all like you," he said wryly. "Perhaps that is just as well. But she is pretty enough in her funny little way. She has black hair and very large brown eyes . . . and a snub nose. The marriage will probably be in the New Year." His face grew grave again. "You do not think too badly of me, *chérie*?"

"You know I don't. I'm very glad this has happened. I was a little afraid that——"

Yves cut her short. "That I would go back to my old ways—yes? Well, I admit I was tempted. But one does not cure a broken heart by getting drunk, or by making love to someone who also has red hair but who is not . . . the one you want. You know, I think my friendship with you has changed me. It no longer seems very amusing to be a gay bachelor without responsibilities." He gave a rather hollow laugh. "This time next year I may even be a papa."

"And just as proud of it as anyone else, I expect," Joanna said lightly.

"But you?" he said, changing the subject. "What about you, *petite*? This unhappiness and depression of which Hugo told me? Was it only nerves before your début?"

Joanna hesitated, half inclined to tell him the truth. But she didn't think he was ready to learn that she was in love with someone else, so she took the cue.

"Yes, it was silly of me, but I was scared to death," she said casually. "Oh, Yves, I'm so sorry Gustave dragged you over here, but it was sweet of you to come."

For an instant, she thought she blundered. His eyes kindled with a glint of repressed passion and he leaned towards her. But, almost at once, he controlled himself and said, equally carelessly, "Well, now at least you have no more to worry about on that score. You are a great success. You know, I cannot get over the fact that you are really English. I would never have guessed it."

"I would have told you if you'd asked." She glanced at

the clock. "Heavens, look at the time! I must get some sleep or I shall look a hag tomorrow."

Yves rose and moved to the door. "You never look a hag, and you know it. Goodbye, my dear. Good luck."

*　　　　*　　　　*

The following morning, Joanna had barely finished breakfast before Gustave burst in. He was even more exuberant than he had been the night before, and was carrying a bundle of national newspapers under his arm.

"You want to know what they think of you? Read those, *chérie!*" he instructed. Then he returned to the sitting-room and proceeded to engage in a series of voluble telephone calls.

Joanna hitched up her pillows, swallowed a couple of aspirins in the hope of dispelling her headache, and searched the papers for the parts he had had circled with red pencil. They were mainly gossip column notes, and some of them carried the photographs which Gustave had had taken on her second day in London.

One writer described her as *the most scintillating new star to appear in the London cabaret firmament for many seasons. She has the glamour of Dietrich, the magnetism of Liza Minelli—and a voice that makes nonsense of the claims to talent of so many of the currently popular recording artists.*

Another, equally extravagant, said: *Not since Shirley Bassey won acclaim at the former Café de Paris has London's jaded night life been invigorated by such a vital new personality as this ravishing French girl who was first discovered in a sleazy Montmartre wine cellar.*

Gustave reappeared in the doorway as she finished reading the last item.

"So? What do you think?" he enquired.

Joanna tossed the pile of papers aside. "I think they must be pretty short of material to make so much of it—and they're not very accurate. That club where you found me wasn't in Montmartre."

He chuckled. "Never mind, it is only a trifling detail. And anyway, Montmartre is still considered the centre of wicked doings by most English people, I believe. However,

I am glad that you do not take them too seriously. It is never wise to believe one's own publicity. The very people who build you up can also destroy you, my pigeon."

Joanna closed her eyes and wished that he would go away and leave her to be wretched in peace.

"By the way, how did it go last night?" he asked curiously. "All is well again now?"

Joanna nodded. It was too much trouble to explain the truth to him, and would only start him fussing over her again.

"As I thought, it is going to be a busy day," Gustave said cheerfully, rustling the pages of a note-pad. "Now this morning you have a fitting for that silver dress and I have also made an appointment at a beauty salon for a massage and manicure. At one, you are lunching at the Caprice with Mr. David Rand. He writes the show business page for the *Daily Globe*. Later you can have a short rest and then you must dress for an interview in the 'Tonight' programme on television. Later in the week there is another lunch with the theatrical columnist from *Vogue*, and they will probably ask you to model some dresses for them. Ah, and there is a second television engagement on the commercial channel."

"In that case I'd better get up," Joanna said, with an attempt to sound brisk and eager.

It was while she was having a bath that she realised she had no idea where Charles and Cathy were staying during their visit. During the night, she had thought that if she could arrange to meet Cathy somewhere, it might lead to one last chance to win back Charles's approval. No man—not even Charles Carlyon—could look at a woman as he had looked at her last night, and a day later be totally indifferent to her. Whatever interpretations he had put on Yves's arrival, there must be some way to make him understand the truth.

The snag was that her day was going to be so full that, even if she could contact Cathy, there would be very little time in which to meet her. And even if she could check at the hundred and one hotels where they might be, there was still the possibility that they might be putting up with some of the many friends and business contacts whom Charles knew in London.

However, in spite of the difficulty she was likely to encounter in tracing them, as soon as her fitting was over Joanna ignored the salon appointment and hurried back to the hotel. For the next hour, until it was time for her to leave for the Caprice, she rang round all the most likely hotels. But none of them had a Mr. Carlyon or a Miss Durrant on their registers, and it was in a very deflated mood that Joanna ordered a taxi and set out for the famous theatrical restaurant.

A few minutes after seven, in a simple black cocktail dress and a valuable diamond necklace which Gustave had borrowed for the occasion, she made her first television appearance on "Tonight." But although it was uncomfortably hot under the battery of lights and the special television make-up made her feel as if she were wearing a mask, it was not the ordeal she had anticipated. The young man who interviewed her seemed friendly and admiring and she was not obliged to deal with any of the barbed questions which Gustave had warned her to parry. Most of the time —and it was over very quickly—she was wondering if Charles or Cathy might be watching.

Later, her performance at the end of the cabaret was as successful as that of the night before. But, to Gustave's annoyance, she refused to sing *Until We Met* again.

The day after that was so hectic that she had no chance to pursue her search for Cathy, and she began to feel that it was a waste of time and nervous energy to try. Anyway, they were probably back in Merefield by now.

It occurred to her suddenly that if she had telephoned Mrs. Howard, she could have obtained their address quite easily. But now that they might be home again, she didn't dare ring Charles's number. It might be his voice that answered her call, and it would be futile to try to soften him over miles of telephone line.

Five days after her début, Joanna was dressing for the cabaret when the telephone rang in the sitting-room. Gustave was there, looking through the proofs of another batch of photographs, and she heard him answer it. As yet, he didn't seem to have noticed that Yves was never about.

171

"It's for you, Janine," he called through the door. Then, as she came into the sitting-room in the silver lamé gown with its hem of fluttering white ostrich feathers, "Don't be too long. You are on in less than ten minutes."

Joanna took the receiver. It was probably the importunate Mr. Rand who, having given her a rave write-up in his show column, was intent on pursuing their acquaintance.

"Hello? Janine Alain speaking," she said impatiently.

"Joanna, this is Charles. Look, I'm sorry to bother you, but I need your help."

"Charles!" Her fingers tightened convulsively on the receiver. "What is it—what's happened?"

"It's Cathy—she's had a slight accident," he said rapidly. "Don't flap. She isn't seriously injured, but she has some concussion."

"Cathy . . . an accident?" Joanna exclaimed, horrified.

"She dashed across Regent Street without looking both ways, silly child," Charles explained. "Fortunately, I was with her, or it might have been hours before we knew about it. Look, the reason I've called you is because she seems to be slightly delirious. She keeps muttering your name and nobody else can comfort her. I wondered if, when your show is over, you could possibly spare half an hour to come round and see her."

"Where are you?" Joanna said quickly.

He gave her the name of the hospital. "I know it will be late and you'll be tired, but——"

"I'll come at once. I'll be there in fifteen minutes," Joanna said decisively. Then she slammed down the receiver, darted back into the bedroom and began struggling with the fastenings of the silver dress.

"Janine! What are you doing? It is nearly time for your entrance," Gustave cried, bewildered.

"There's been an accident. I have to go to the hospital." The zip-fastener stuck and Joanna tugged at it for some seconds, then gripped the material and wrenched out the interlocking teeth.

"What accident? What hospital? You must be out of your mind!"

172

"Perhaps I am. I don't care. You'll just have to make some excuse." She pulled open the wardrobe and grabbed a plain cotton day dress. "I'm sorry, Gustave—but this is something important."

"Important!" he exploded. "What is more important than your career? If you disappear now—within seconds of your entrance—your whole future may be wrecked."

Joanna thrust her arms into the sleeves of a light wool coat, seized her bag and turned towards the door. Then, realising she was still wearing the high-heeled *pointelle* slippers that went with the silver dress, she kicked them off and rummaged for leather flatties.

"I can't help that, Gustave. This is vital. You'll have to tell them I'm ill or something."

The shoes were on her feet and she was ready to go, but Gustave seized her arm. "But you are not ill," he said fiercely "—unless you are deranged. Nothing—*nothing* can be more important to you than your professional reputation. Always your career must come first."

Joanna looked at him coldly. "You mean 'the show must go on'?" she said icily.

"Exactly so. It is one of the first precepts of——"

"Then it will have to go on without me, because I'm not that kind of careerist," she retorted. "No show on earth is so important that it comes before human beings who need you."

And wrenching out of his grasp, she fled to the outer door and down the corridor.

*   *   *

An hour later, a pleasant-faced young man in a white coat came softly into the dimly-lit side ward where Joanna was sitting by a bed. Cathy was asleep now, her small face pinched and pale, her left hand clasped round Joanna's.

"I think she'll sleep for several hours now," he said in a low voice. "You must be pretty tired yourself, Miss . . . ?"

"Allen," Joanna supplied. Gently, she loosed Cathy's fingers and laid them on the sheet.

In the corridor, the doctor indicated the way to the lift. He had met her and exchanged a few words before she had been shown into Cathy's room, but this seemed to be the first time he had noticed the heavy stage make-up she was wearing. He studied her face for a moment, his eyebrows contracting.

"We haven't met before, have we?" as they reached the lift.

Joanna shook her head. "I'm a singer. You might possibly have seen me on television a few nights ago."

"Good lord—yes, I remember now. But I thought you were French," he said, puzzled.

"I am—in a way. Doctor, Cathy is going to be all right, isn't she?"

"Yes, of course. There's no need for you to worry about her. A few days' rest and she'll be as right as ninepence. But if you could pop in tomorrow morning—she seems very attached to you."

"I'll come," Joanna promised. "And thank you for all you're doing for her." The lift arrived and she stepped into it.

"Oh, by the way, the chap who came in with her—her cousin, I believe he said—is still downstairs in the waiting-room. Ground floor, turn left and you'll see the notice over the door." The doctor pressed the button for her, waved a cheerful farewell and went on his way.

Charles was leaning on the radiator when Joanna entered the waiting-room. He straightened and looked at her enquiringly.

"She's fast asleep. The doctor says we needn't worry," Joanna said quickly.

"Thank God for that." Charles ran a hand over his head and relaxed. "This place is like a hot-house. Let's go out to the car."

It had been raining, and the night air was cool and sweet. Somewhere a clock struck midnight.

"It was good of you to come," Charles said formally, as they walked round to the car park.

"You must have known I would."

"Well, yes, but I didn't think you'd be able to get here so quickly. You're not working tonight, I gather."

"I was supposed to be," she said.

He didn't react for a moment, then he caught her elbow and swung her round to face him.

"You mean you didn't appear? You just walked out and left them standing?"

"That's right." She echoed Gustave. "I'm afraid I broke one of the first precepts of the theatre—'the show must go on.' Don't tell me you disapprove too. Gustave was furious, of course, but then he's in the business."

"Disapprove!" Charles sounded oddly hoarse. "But this could be taken as a breach of contract, couldn't it? They could kick you out."

"If they chose to be awkward, I suppose they could," she agreed, with a slight shrug.

Charles was still holding her elbow. "You mean you risked losing your job for Cathy?"

Joanna raised her face to his. "Not entirely for Cathy," she said quietly. "You sounded so worried, Charles. I thought it might help to have . . . another member of the family on hand."

His fingers bit into her arm. "Oh, God!" he said huskily. "Joanna, I——" Then his arms were round her and he was kissing her with a passion that left no doubt how he felt about her.

They were standing in the opening to the car-park, and the next thing Joanna knew was that a beam of bright light was shining against her closed lids. Then Charles raised his head, muttered an expletive and drew her a yard to one side. The car which they had been impeding edged slowly forward. As it drew abreast, the unseen driver gave vent to a long low whistle. With a smothered laugh, Charles drew her back into his arms and kissed her again.

"This does mean what I hope it means, doesn't it?" he enquired presently, his lips against her temple.

Joanna drew a long quivering breath. She felt rather as if she had just been through a whirlwind, but the sensation was far from unpleasant.

"What do you hope it means?" she asked, in a small voice.

175

"That you love me—that you'll marry me?"

"Oh, Charles, you must know I do—and will."

His arms tightened, but this time he did not kiss her. "I don't know why I should," he said ruefully. "Up till tonight you've been markedly offhand, my sweet."

"Only because I didn't know how *you* felt. It isn't 'done' for women to show their feelings."

"Maybe not, but they can drop the odd hint, can't they?"

"But I *did*—dozens. The other night at the hotel——"

"Yes, I must admit you did seem quite pleased to see me. But it was a bit of a setback—that French chap showing up."

"Oh, Charles, you weren't really jealous of poor Yves? He's never meant anything to me—at least not in this way. And he's engaged to someone else."

"Was he engaged to someone else that night at the Cordiale?"

"No, not then—or he wouldn't have been trying to kiss me. It—it's all rather complicated. Do I have to explain it now?"

"No, for the moment there are more important topics. Look, we can't stand here much longer. Let's get in the car. It's starting to rain again and I want to kiss you in comfort."

Some time later, when her heart had settled down to an approximately regular beat, Joanna moved her head against Charles's shoulder. "But if you felt . . . like this, I don't understand why you were so beastly to me," she murmured. "Well, not beastly perhaps—but not in the least lover-like."

He caressed her cheek with his knuckles. "There were several reasons. The chief obstacle—and it still stands, I'm afraid—is that I felt it was wrong to ask you to make such a sacrifice."

"What sacrifice?" she asked blankly.

He withdrew his arm from around her and lit a cigarette. "We have to be realistic, Joanna," he said seriously, reaching for a cigarette. "I'm not the kind of man who can play second fiddle, and you haven't worked all these years and finally got where you are just to throw it all over and become a provincial housewife. If I hadn't been . . . pretty keyed up this evening, I wouldn't have let this happen."

His reasoning seemed so fantastic to her that, for some seconds, Joanna couldn't speak. Then she said furiously, "So you'd have let me go on thinking you despised me, and ruined both our lives? Oh, you Englishmen are incredible! Thank goodness Frenchmen aren't so stupidly noble."

"You hot-tempered little idiot! Don't you see——"

Joanna slid her arms round his neck and pressed her mouth against his. She felt him stiffen, but it was only momentary, and then his arm gripped her fiercely round the waist. In the end, it was she who had to beg to be allowed to catch her breath.

His hold slackened. "But what does that prove?" he asked thickly.

"That you can't resist me indefinitely . . . and that I know what I want out of life," she whispered huskily. "Oh, Charles, don't you see? It wouldn't *be* a sacrifice. It would be a wonderful exchange. A career isn't what I want. It was only a substitute for the things that really matter to a woman—love, and a home and children. I don't even have to think about it, my darling."

"You're sure—you're very sure?"

She gave a low laugh. "Shall I tell you something? When I had to come to London, I wasn't excited and pleased. I was utterly miserable because I thought I'd never see you again. And the other night . . . I didn't care if the rest of the audience liked me . . . I was singing for you. Oh, please, I've been lonely for so long—don't take this away because you have silly doubts. All I ever want is to be yours—to belong to you."

He took her face between his hands. "I believe you mean that. But, my love, have you really considered what you will be giving up?"

She turned her lips into his palm. "Fame, money, luxury —they don't make up happiness, Charles. I think they probably destroy it, or at least make it very difficult to find. Oh, yes, every woman dreams of having wonderful clothes and being admired and fêted. But we don't *need* that, darling—and we do need love, terribly."

There was a moment's pause and then he bent his head and lightly kissed her forehead. "All right, you win, my sweet. But when you're a harried wife with a couple of infants at your apron-strings, don't come to me for sympathy. Once you're mine, you're mine till you drop."

Joanna drew a deep breath. "It sounds heavenly." She pushed back her tumbled hair. "And now, I suppose, I'd better get back and face the music. But it doesn't really matter if they *do* sack me now, does it?"

"I hope they will, then we can get married right away." Charles gave her a reassuring pat. "Don't panic, sweetheart. They won't eat you while I'm around."

*　　　*　　　*

A little after ten o'clock the following morning, Charles's car drew up at the entrance to the hotel and Joanna slid into the passenger seat. They were going to see Cathy and break their news.

"Seen Hugo this morning?" Charles asked, when they were merging with the traffic.

"Mm, I've just left him. He's still furious, of course, but you know I have a suspicion that it's fifty per cent put on. He was really angry last night—and I suppose he was justified, in a way. I owe everything to him—including you, since he advised me to come to England with you—and my defections reflect on him to some extent. But under that hard-bitten exterior I believe he's really rather romantic. I think he's beginning to regard my retirement as a kind of *crime passionel*—shocking but excusable."

"Perhaps he's another of your victims, my pet?"

"Gustave?" she expostulated. "Oh, Charles, don't be absurd. He's old enough to be my father—older—and he isn't as soft-boiled as all that." Her eyes lingered on his strong profile. Now, at last, she could look at him without the fear that he might suddenly turn his head and read the expression on her face. "Charles, when did you begin to love me?"

He laughed. "I wonder if there's any woman alive who hasn't asked that question? Is it so vital to know when the fish was hooked?" Then, serious again, "I was always attracted to you, but I think I first realised it was serious on the night of that party. When I saw you wandering

178

about the garden with young Neal, I could have flattened him."

"Yes, I was always attracted to you in a reluctant kind of way," she admitted. "I wonder what Cathy will say?"

"I suspect she'll approve. Ever since I hustled her out of the hotel the other night, she's been alternately glowering at me, or pointing out all your good qualities."

"If it hadn't been for her we should still be miserable," Joanna said gratefully.

She told Cathy so at the end of their visit. Charles had left them alone for the last few moments while he had a word with the doctor.

"I say, Joanna—I don't want to sound madly self-centred, but you won't be so taken up with getting married that you'll forget to put in a good word for me, will you?" Cathy asked diffidently, just before they said goodbye.

As Charles had forecast, she had been overjoyed to learn that they were engaged, and was already fretting to leave the hospital where she was missing all the excitement. Although, as Joanna had told her, since the management of the hotel had not sacked her after all, she would have to work out her contract before she and Charles could be married.

"A good word?" Joanna asked. "Oh, you mean about taking up acting. Well, I'll certainly do my best for you, pet." She grinned. "Charles does seem exceptionally mellow at the moment."

"So he jolly well ought to be," Cathy declared. "Do you know the *Daily Mirror* describes you as 'the most luscious French import since Brigitte Bardot'?"

"I think that's vaguely libellous," Joanna said, laughing. "My voice is my fortune, not my bosom."

Cathy caught her hand. "I say, Jo, if I tell you something, will you swear not to let on?"

"I think I can guess—you've fallen wildly in love with that nice young doctor."

"No, nothing like that—although he is rather blissful, isn't he?" Cathy agreed. "No, this is just to prove that I'm a pretty good actress already. You see"—she glanced nervously at the door "—although I did feel pretty ghastly last night, I wasn't really rambling. You see, I knew Charles was absolutely potty about you, and I guessed how you felt about him, so I thought if I kept moaning your name, they'd fetch you here. And it worked, didn't it?"

Joanna wasn't sure whether to laugh or be horrified. "Oh, darling, I don't think you ought to have pretended to be worse than you were—but yes, it did work wonders."

"Well, I had to do *something*. Charles had been behaving like an ogre all the week, and anyway I wanted to keep you with us. Do you suppose I can live with you—just until I start training—or would I be a terrible gooseberry?"

"We like gooseberries." Joanna bent and kissed her. "Now I must fly, pet. We're going to choose a ring. 'Bye —see you later!"

Charles was standing at the far end of the corridor as she closed the door behind her. Walking towards him, Joanna knew that all the best in her life was just beginning.

January Paperbacks

THAT SUMMER OF SURRENDER
Rebecca Caine

After her father's death Perdita's happy relationship with
Olivia, her stepmother, had brought no problems. But when
Olivia had the chance of making a new life for herself
Perdita found herself dealing with considerable difficulties—
not the least of which was the arrival on the scene of the
insufferable Blake Hadwyn!

LOVE AND LUCY BROWN
Joyce Dingwell

Lucy was delighted when a kindly lady arranged a job for
her in a hospital-cum-children's home in Australia, and
could hardly wait to get to Sydney and start her fascinating
new job. But she arrived to find herself rather less than
welcome to the doctor in charge, Tavis Walsh—and still less
to the glamorous Sister Ursula!

DARLING JENNY
Janet Dailey

Jennifer Glenn, smarting from a disastrous love affair with
Brad Stevenson, had taken herself off to the skiing grounds
of Wyoming to 'get away from it all' and lend a hand to her
busy sister Sheila at the same time. She never expected to
fall in love again almost at once—and certainly not with the
man who was in love with Sheila!

THE IMPOSSIBLE MARRIAGE
Lilian Peake

Old Mrs. Dunlopp thought it was a splendid idea to leave
her large house and a lot of money to her great-nephew
Grant Gard and her young friend Beverley Redmund—on
condition that within six months they got married. There was
one snag: the two people concerned just couldn't stand each
other!

AUTUMN CONCERTO
Rebecca Stratton

It was through the attractive young Frenchman Jacques
Delange that Ruth had lost her job, so it was really the least
that Jacques could do to find her another—working for
his uncle Hugo. But Hugo Gerard was to cause Ruth
considerably more heart-searching than his nephew!

25p net each

January Paperbacks *continued*

THE NOBLE SAVAGE
Violet Winspear

The rich, appallingly snobbish Mrs. Amy du Mont would have given almost anything to be admitted to the society of the imposing Conde Estuardo Santigardas de Reyes. But it was Mrs. du Mont's quiet, shy little companion who interested the Conde...

PROUD CITADEL
Elizabeth Hoy

Judy had burned her boats by coming out to Morocco to marry Glen Grant, against the wishes of her family. But it was another woman who was going to present the biggest threat to Judy's marriage...

WHITE HEAT
Pamela Kent

The voyage out to Australia was fun for Karin, except for the ruthlessness of Kent Willoughby—until the ship caught fire and Karin was cast adrift in the Indian Ocean with only a manservant and Kent himself.

A PAVEMENT OF PEARL
Iris Danbury

Rianna accompanied her brother to Sicily to join an underwater expedition in the hope of finding something of interest for a travel article she intended to write. But the uncompromising Holford Sinclair, leader of the expedition, made it clear that he had no time for Rianna's interference in his work. How dared he treat her like this?

HIGH-COUNTRY WIFE
Gloria Bevan

Rosanne enjoyed her work as nursery nurse aboard ship until she committed the fatal mistake of becoming too involved in the future of one of her charges, four-year-old Nicky. It was a mistake which led her into marriage with the disturbingly attractive Craig Houston, a man who felt nothing for her. Yet...

25p net each

February Paperbacks

THE GILDED BUTTERFLY
Elizabeth Ashton

Alastair Grainger had saved Selina from an unpleasant and dangerous situation, so perhaps it was inevitable that she should have fallen in love with him. But he was not for her, he told her firmly; she must go away and forget him. Was it going to be as easy as that, though?

HEAVEN IS GENTLE
Betty Neels

Professor Christian van Duyl was a formidable character, but it didn't take Sister Eliza Proudfoot long to fall in love with him. And a great waste of time *that* was going to be, since the Professor was shortly to be married to the so suitable Estelle. Or *was* she so suitable?

FOOD FOR LOVE
Rachel Lindsay

Amanda could see problems ahead when her boss, Clive Rand, began taking a serious interest in her, so she changed her job. And found still more problems in the person of that mysterious, maddening man, Red Clark!

THE DREAM ON THE HILL
Lilian Peake

Nicola Dean and Connor Mitchell had both curtailed promising careers in order to help their parents, so they ought to have had a lot in common. Unfortunately, they just couldn't stand the sight of each other!

GATE OF THE GOLDEN GAZELLE
Dorothy Cook·

Natalie Jones had got herself into a rather complicated and mysterious situation in Morocco—and somehow she persuaded her friend Josian Jones to take her place. Which led Josian into a lot of adventures—with or without the disturbing Raymond Laurent!

25p net each

February Paperbacks *continued*

THE SWALLOWS OF SAN FEDORA
Betty Beaty

As an air hostess Emma was accustomed to dealing with almost any awkward situation, but her assignment in Sicily seemed to be proving more than usually problem-filled. Besides the difficulties brought by the passengers there was the autocratic captain of the aircraft, Mark Creighton, a man who seemed determined to put Emma in the wrong. What should she do?

THE KISSING GATE
Joyce Dingwell

'See me when you grow up,' Clem had told Silver when she was little more than a child. Now she was a woman and returned to the place where she had spent her childhood. Would Clem remember those happy times? Did Silver really care whether he did or not?

DESIGN FOR DESTINY
Sue Peters

Because she felt partly responsible for the accident which had injured Ryan St. John, Jan offered her help in looking after his young nephew. It would not be long before the domineering Ryan was fit again and she could return to her job in London as designer for a leading fashion house. But when the time came for her to leave Jan found herself strangely reluctant to go . . .

DANGEROUS RHAPSODY
Anne Mather

Emma's job in the Bahamas was not as glamorous as it seemed—for her employer, Damon Thorne, had known her before—and as time went on she realised that he was bent on using her to satisfy some strange and incomprehensible desire for vengeance . . .

THE FARAWAY BRIDE
Linden Grierson

Janet Cook had married Neil Stonham—and gone off to Australia with him—to get away from her dreary life. He had married her to put a stop to his meddling aunt's match-making. But could they make each other happy?

25p net each

March Paperbacks

DARK VIKING
Mary Wibberley

When Emma inherited a cottage in the Shetlands she had looked forward to escaping for a while from the hectic world of modelling. But when she finally travelled northwards she was to find that the peace and quiet for which she had longed were impossible in the presence of her new neighbour, the aggressive Greg Halcro.

RETURN TO DEEPWATER
Lucy Gillen

As a child Tarin had hero-worshipped Darrel Bruce. Now, when she encountered him again, she found a brusque and arrogant businessman, though still with a disturbing attraction for her. But what right had Tarin to his love when the sophisticated Gloria Stein wanted to stake her claim?

WHERE THE MOONFLOWER WEAVES
Roumelia Lane

Judi's first encounter with the aggressive Blake Morrison was not a happy one she resolved to have as few dealings with him as possible. Which was an unfortunate decision to take considering that she was to be forced to spend three weeks with him trekking through the jungle forests of Ceylon! Soon Judi was to reconsider her attitude towards Blake. But what of him?

THE BRIDE PRICE
Elizabeth Hunter

Celia Sterling had led a sheltered life with her grandfather on his farm in Kenya. Her peace was shattered by the arrival of Julian Fairburn, who presented her grandfather with the tusks of a rogue elephant, so that she thought the ivory was a bride price and that the time would come when he would return to claim her for his wife . . .

COUNTRY OF THE FALCON
Anne Mather

When Alexandra went to the uncivilised regions of the Amazon to look for her father, she was prepared to find life different from the security of her English home. She certainly didn't expect, however, to find herself at the mercy of the dangerously attractive Declan O'Rourke and to be forced to accompany him to his mountain retreat at Paradiablo.

25p net each

March Paperbacks *continued*

STRANGER IN THE GLEN
Flora Kidd

Jan had sampled life in a big city and had decided that it was not for her. She returned to the peace of her family's home at Tighnacoarach to help with the sheep. But she was to find that her meeting with the stranger, Duncan, brought unrest into her thoughts. Who exactly was he, and what did he want in the glen?

RIDE OUT THE STORM
Jane Donnelly

Priscilla took an instant dislike to the stranger Jason Wyatt, before she was even aware of how he threatened her happiness and that of her family. Yet she found their constant battles bringing a new excitement to her life. Could it be that Jason meant more to her than she realised? What would Allan think about it all?

MOONRISE OVER THE MOUNTAINS
Lilian Peake

When Ewan Pascall offered Gayle a job within his organisation which carried greater responsibilities she took up the challenge, although she realised that her attempts were bound to result in failure. At least that would mean that she would never meet the autocratic Ewan again. But was that what Gayle really wanted?

TEMPESTUOUS APRIL
Betty Neels

It was when Nurse Harriet's Dutch friend, Sieske, invited Harriet home that she caught up with a dream from her past—the man she had always hoped to marry. Harriet was to find, however, that she was not alone in having this dream—and that the man in question had a reputation for liking pretty girls!

THE ADVENTURESOME SPIRIT
Linden Grierson

Mary had set off for an adventurous holiday across Australia, but instead found herself posing as John Parvue's fiancée in his family's home. Which was quite complicated enough, even before she fell foul of John's disapproving brother Peter!

25p net each

DID YOU MISS OUR 1974 CHRISTMAS PACK?

THE JAPANESE SCREEN
Anne Mather

Susannah met and fell in love with **Fernando Cuevas in** London. She little thought when she travelled to Spain to work for a wealthy family that the child she had come to teach was Fernando's child and that she would be meeting Fernando himself sooner than she had expected . . .

THE GIRL AT GOLDENHAWK
Violet Winspear

Jaine was accustomed always to take back place to her aunt, a spoilt darling of the London stage, and her glamorous cousin Laraine. As it seemed only natural to *them* that Jaine should take on the difficult task of explaining to Laraine's wealthy suitor that she had changed her mind about the marriage, Jaine nerved herself to meet the arrogant Pedro de Ros Zanto. Was there a surprise in store?

PRIDE AND POWER
Anne Hampson

Leona's pride suffered a tremendous blow when she discovered that the beautiful mansion and the prosperous farm that went with it belonged not as she thought to her grandmother, but to the forbidding Konon Wyndham, a man she had always hated. Now he had the power to humble her. Would he use it?

SWEET SUNDOWN
Margaret Way

Ever since she was a little girl Gabriele had been promised a trip to Sundown, the lovely old mansion where her mother had been born. And now she was going there at last at the invitation of her glamorous aunt Camilla. What would the visit bring Gabriele in the way of a new life . . . and a new love?

Available at £1.00 net per pack
either from your local bookshop or if in difficulty from
Mills & Boon Reader Service,
P.O. Box 236, 14 Sanderstead Rd.,
S. Croydon, CR2 OYG, Surrey, England.

Your Astral Guide

Specially written for Mills & Boon readers, this series of paperbacks is a must for every woman who needs to know the facts about the men in her life (husbands, boy-friends and bosses).

There is one book for each star sign - from Leo to Libra - from Aries to Aquarius.

Unlike other horoscopes - which just give endless pages of predictions - these invaluable little books give vital information on how to deal with your man.

*Do Taureans make good lovers?

*Are Cancerians too home-loving?

*Could *you* tame a Leo?

*What influence does the ascendant sign have on your man's character?

You can find out all this and more. Each book is packed with information drawings and charts, and only 35p.

12 books in the series coming in the autumn

ARIES	LIBRA
TAURUS	SCORPIO
GEMINI	SAGITTARIUS
CANCER	CAPRICORN
LEO	AQUARIUS
VIRGO	PISCES

If you have difficulty in obtaining copies of these books from your local stockist, please wtite to
MILLS & BOON READER SERVICE,
P.O. Box 236, 14 Sanderstead Road, S. Croydon, CR2 0YG, England, enclosing 35p plus 2p per book for postage and packing.

Your copy of the Mills & Boon Magazine — 'Happy Reading'

If you enjoyed reading this MILLS & BOON romance and would like a list of other MILLS & BOON romances available, together with details of all future publications and special offers, why not fill in the coupon below and you will receive, by return and post free, your own copy of the MILLS & BOON magazine —'*Happy Reading*'.

Not only does it list nearly 400 MILLS & BOON romances which are available either from your local bookshop or in case of difficulty from MILLS & BOON READER SERVICE, P.O. BOX 236, 14 Sanderstead Road, S. Croydon, CR2 OYG, Surrey, England, but it also includes articles on cookery and craft, a pen-pals scheme, letters from overseas readers, plus an exciting competition!

For those of you who can't wait to receive our catalogue we have listed over the page a selection of current titles. This list may include titles you have missed or had difficulty in obtaining from your usual stockist. Just tick the selection your require, fill in the coupon below and send the whole page to us with your remittance including postage and packing. We will despatch your order to you by return!

Please send me the free MILLS & BOON magazine ☐
Please send me the titles ticked ☐

I enclose £   (No C.O.D.) Please add 2p per book for postage and packing (10p if you live outside the U.K.)

Name ....Miss/Mrs.

Address ....

City/Town ....

County/Country ....Postal/Zip Code..............

MB 12/74

Your Mills & Boon Selection

☐ 615
THE OTHER TURNER GIRL
Ruth Clemence

☐ 635
IMMORTAL FLOWER
Elizabeth Hoy

☐ 656
THE MILL IN THE MEADOW
Jane Donnelly

☐ 665
IF LOVE BE LOVE
Flora Kidd

☐ 688
HAPPY WITH EITHER
Ruth Clemence

☐ 757
THE ONE AND ONLY
Doris E. Smith

☐ 764
AN ECHO OF SPRING
Lucy Gillen

☐ 778
FAMILIAR STRANGER
Lilian Peake

☐ 789
WHITE HUNTER
Elizabeth Hoy

☐ 798
ERRANT BRIDE
Elizabeth Ashton

☐ 801
A SONG BEGINS
Mary Burchell

☐ 807A
ROMAN SUMMER
Jane Arbor

☐ 809
WINTER OF CHANGE
Betty Neels

☐ 812
BELOVED ENEMY
Mary Wibberley

☐ 815
THE YOUNG DOCTOR
Sheila Douglas

☐ 817
WINDWARD CREST
Anne Hampson

☐ 825
THE CRESCENT MOON
Elizabeth Hunter

☐ 827
BEWILDERED HEART
Kathryn Blair

☐ 834
MIRANDA'S MARRIAGE
Margery Hilton

☐ 839
STARS THROUGH THE MIST
Betty Neels

☐ 841
THE NIGHT OF THE HURRICANE
Andrea Blake

☐ 852
STORM OVER MANDARGI
Margaret Way

☐ 857
LUCIFER'S ANGEL
Violet Winspear

☐ 863
CINDERELLA IN MINK
Roberta Leigh

☐ 868
THE HONEY IS BITTER
Violet Winspear

All priced at 20p. Please tick your requirements and
see over for handy order form.